SPEAK OF ME AS I AM

~~~

Sonia Belasco

Philomel Books

PHILOMEL BOOKS
an imprint of Penguin Random House LLC
375 Hudson Street, New York, NY 10014

Library of Congress Cataloging-in-Publication Data
Names: Belasco, Sonia, author. | Title: Speak of me as I am / Sonia Belasco. |
Description: New York, NY : Philomel Books, 2017. | Summary: Damon and
Melanie, two teenagers who have lost loved ones, meet and help each other
grieve, but as their friendship deepens into romance, things get complicated
fast. | Identifiers: LCCN 2016003297 | ISBN 9780399546761
Subjects: | CYAC: Grief—Fiction. | Love—Fiction. | Classification: LCC
PZ7.1.B4458 Sp 2017 | DDC [Fic]—dc23
LC record available at https://lccn.loc.gov/2016003297

Printed in the United States of America.
ISBN 9780399546761
1 3 5 7 9 10 8 6 4 2

Edited by Talia Benamy.   Design by Semadar Megged.
Text set in 11-point Berling LT Std.

for Etta

DAMON

I keep thinking about that time we went to that
carnival—the one in Virginia with the crazy-ass
ride that spun you upside down and held you there?
You called me a pussy because I wouldn't go on it.
It was like—dude, I like excitement, I do, but life is
exciting enough for me without vomiting. That is
all I was trying to say.
I think maybe I was never exciting enough for you, that
I held you back. You were brave. You always went
after what you wanted.
But if you'd wanted that, if you—even if you just wanted
to talk about it? I would have listened.
Even if I couldn't—
You were my best friend, man.

CHAPTER ONE

I don't know how I ended up here today. It's all a blur—so many houses and people, buses and dogs and stores and sidewalks, car horns and lawns and, above it all, the soft blue of the late summer sky.

Now I'm here.

I'm here again.

All I see is green. Oak and maple trees rise over my head, melting into evergreens that nearly block out the sun. The branches overlap like hands with fingers laced together. The sun penetrates and prickles the ground with light, dots here and there, leaving the mossy ground cover studded with stars.

I lift the camera toward the sky, frame the trees and snap.

Freeze.

I turn the camera over in my hands. I can see Carlos's hands, his nails short and bitten down, skin dry, knuckles white but fingers so sure on the buttons. My hands are different—my skin a darker brown, fingers longer and more tapered. My hands look different curved around the camera: not as natural.

The camera always looked like it belonged in Carlos's hands, like they'd been shaped around it. He'd snap a picture and I wouldn't even realize he'd done it because his motions were so swift, the machine an extension of his body, another limb.

I click over to a photo of a stone statue of a woman draped in robes and a long head covering, seated in front of the National Archives. There's a solemn, simple message etched into the base below her sandal-clad feet: *WHAT IS PAST IS PROLOGUE.*

I can see green, and my own hand, reaching out—

I exhale and turn.

Jesus.

I suck in a breath.

I see *her.*

This is the first time I've ever seen someone else here. She's hard *not* to see with her hair streaked candy-apple red, a whole bunch of piercings in her ears, ripped jeans and a black T-shirt that proclaims *Hard to Handle* in large bubble letters.

I could believe that. I could believe she's hard to handle.

She's sitting on the ground leaning against that tree.

It's that tree. It's that same damn tree.

Oh God, she's crying. Makeup runs down her cheeks. Her shoulders shake. She hugs her knees in closer, pushing back against the rough bark of the tree like she's trying to topple it.

I lift the camera and take her picture.

Freeze.

Why did I do that?

She doesn't move and doesn't register my movement.

I turn to go.

I can't let her see me. She'll think—

What am I doing? Am I just going to take her picture and leave like a creepy—

I clear my throat.

She looks up.

Shit.

"Are you okay?" I ask.

"What?" she asks, her voice high and strangled.

"Are you okay?" I repeat, stepping forward.

"Who are you?" she asks.

"Are you . . ." I start again.

"I'm fine," she says.

"You're crying," I say, Captain Obvious. "Are you sure you're—"

"Who are you?" she asks again.

I get distracted by a rustling in the trees. I look over her shoulder. If I squint, it's like I can still see—

She turns around to see what's behind her, then glances back at me with raised eyebrows. "Are *you* okay?"

"I'm—" I start to say, but stop. "I'm sorry. I'm really sorry. I'm going to go."

I back away, stumbling as I go. My camera bag bounces against my hip, and my shoes make crunching sounds on the ground.

I don't exhale until I'm out of the woods. My heart is thrumming in my throat.

Idiot. I'm an *idiot.*

I lift the camera and stare at the photo captured on the tiny screen. She's pretty up close and in focus—eyes dark and still.

She'd been crying, and I took her picture anyway.

Why did I let her see me?

What did she see?

The walls of my new bedroom are covered with Carlos's photographs. The photos were the first thing I unpacked after we moved here a month ago, before my clothes, before my books, before my toothbrush. I lie back on the bed and let my eyes drift. There's a languid sunset on the beach in North Carolina, the river frozen over in Boston, Atlanta's hiccuping bar graph of a skyline. Trips we took together, mostly, because Carlos's family never went anywhere, never had any money to go, never wanted to spend more time together than they had to.

There are my parents, laughing as they share a huge tropical drink that's sprouted about ten tiny umbrellas. There's my grandmother, dressed for church in a pastel flower-patterned suit and scary huge Sunday hat, looking at the camera steadily over the rims of her bifocals. There are landscapes and portraits and candids and even weird arty abstracts, in black and white and full color and soft sepia tones, all captured with Carlos's careful hands.

You're always watching, I told him once. *Freak.*

Yeah, well, Carlos said, tiny bracket lines forming at the corners of his eyes. *You're just so good to look at, homeboy.*

I crossed my eyes at him and Carlos laughed, short and loud, an exclamation point.

Carlos and I became friends in preschool after Carlos stole one of my trucks and refused to give it back. My parents had only just taught me about sharing, so I let Carlos have the truck.

You don't want it back? Carlos asked.

I shook my head, even though I did want that truck. Of course I did. I wanted it a lot. It was shiny and red and could go really fast. But I let Carlos have it, because Carlos wanted it more.

Okay, Carlos said, finally. *We can play with it together, I guess.*

I don't even know why I try to mess with your Zen Buddha thing, man, Carlos said to me once. *You're like some kind of mental ninja.*

Man, Carlos. He knew me, but he didn't know everything.

I just wish I could tell him. I wish I could tell him how wrong he was.

But I can't.

When I think of Carlos now, I don't see the solemn, pale boy in the dark suit in that coffin, arms arranged across his chest. I see Carlos, grinning maniacally and wiping his hands on my shirt, leaving his oily prints on the fabric. I see myself shoving Carlos away, saying, *Douchebag, you douchebag!*

I like it that way, man, it's better, Carlos assured me. *Look, I fixed your ugly shirt.*

I'll fix your ugly face, I said, and Carlos laughed a fake laugh, loud and mocking.

I'll fix your mother's ugly—

Oh, shut up, you asshole, I cut him off. *When's the movie, anyway? We gonna miss it 'cause you had to have your nasty-ass chili cheese fries?*

We got half an hour. Relax, cabrón. *Jesus, you worry more than my mother.*

You give your mother a lot to worry about.

Carlos snorted. *She worries 'cause she wants to worry, man.*

No, she worries 'cause you got yourself arrested, pendejo.

Carlos waved his hand. *Whatever, whatever. Stupid shit, indecent exposure, what is that? Wasn't nothing indecent about it.*

You can't just fuck a girl in public because you want to, I said.

Why not? Make love, not war, yeah? Why the hell not?

Why the hell not. That's what Carlos always used to say. I used to kind of envy Carlos—how casual he was about girls, how they never seemed to make him nervous. He'd dated a rainbow of girls, open to it if any of them showed the slightest interest in him: ones with long hair, short hair, straight hair, curly hair, high cheekbones, apple cheeks, round faces, round bodies, skinny chicks, tall girls, short girls, everything in between.

He never stayed with any of them for long, though. *I'm not about that life*, he said once, and I laughed at him and asked, *What, you're not about falling in love?*

Too much drama, he said, and then looked away and changed the subject like he'd said too much.

I remember that day in eighth grade when I told Carlos my parents wanted to send me to Gate Prep. I remember sitting on his front porch and watching the way he tossed a soccer ball up into the air and caught it, over and over again. *Hey*, I said. *I know it's like a private school or whatever, but it could be good, right?*

Carlos turned to look at me with dark eyes, so focused. *They have scholarships and shit?* Carlos said. *I mean, private school kids are bullshit, but I guess it could be all right if we do it together.*

The door of my room cracks open, and I suck in a breath, pulled fast into the present. My mom sticks her head in.

"Hey, sweetie," she says. "I got this for you."

Her dark curls bob as she hands me a small paperback book. I turn it over. It's a copy of *Othello*.

"They're doing it as the fall play at Hamilton," she explains.

My mom has taken it upon herself to do investigative research into my new high school, and she's been peppering me with information all summer. I know she's trying to get me excited about the upcoming school year, but all talk of school makes me want to hit something. Yeah, no more Gate, I get it. Gate without Carlos would be—whatever. It would be haunted hallways, a bunch of kids who didn't really know him but would all have something to say about him anyway.

But Hamilton . . . High school is still high school, man. There is nothing to be excited about.

"So?" I say.

My mom gives me a look, her hand coming to rest on one hip.

"I thought you might be interested in trying out for it, sweetie."

We did August Wilson's *Fences* last fall at Gate Prep. I auditioned on a whim and got the lead: Troy Maxson, the disillusioned dreamer.

I like you, Damon, my director told me. *You're smart up there onstage. You don't fake it.*

I turn the book over in my hand, thinking about what I remember from reading it a few years ago in English: *Othello, the green-eyed monster play.* The Moorish soldier prince, the outsider who marries a white girl and then kills her when his supposed best friend Iago convinces him she's been unfaithful.

Definitely an upper.

"Are you going to do crew?" my mom asks. "Hamilton's got a team. They're pretty good, I think."

I rub at my eyes. "No," I say. "I don't think so."

Not without—

I remember the day I came home from school with a permission slip and a smug smile, thrusting it into my father's hands.

Crew, my dad said, eyebrows jumping up his forehead like spastic moths. *You want to do crew?*

I've never been much of an athlete; yeah, I enjoy the simple, solitary pleasures of running, the ache and strain in my thighs and calves, the air streaming past my ears, but I never had any desire to be on a team, to play games, to win. Yet as I stood on the edge of the Potomac River and watched those rowers slice through the water with precise, snapping strokes, I felt something swell inside of me.

There's water, I thought, *and I want to be on it.*

So it meant being the only black boy amongst a bunch of loud, puffed-up white boys. So what? I could deal when that asshole Brad leaned over during a pre-practice pep talk in the locker room and said, *Basketball team all full up, D?* I'm used to that shit.

I wasn't used to the pain, though. Crew was fucking hard—it was early mornings and long hours, it was blisters on my knuckles and palms, it was red crescent marks on the backs of my calves where the wood from the sliding benches bit into thin skin. It was thirteen-mile runs, and burning in my chest that never stopped, and gasping and panting and stomach clenching. It was running stairs for three hours until I puked behind the bleachers.

It was not being good enough, being singled out, being exhausted, feeling stupid, losing.

But crew was also the sun rising over the river, streaking the sky with splashes of color like a kid with finger paints. Crew was being up so early, I got to eat in complete solitude, the only sound the hollow chirp of crickets and the whir of passing buses. Crew was those moments when every member of the team would suddenly be in sync, all pushing and pulling toward the same goal, the shouting of the cox-swain a thumping, steady rhythm.

Crew was something I did with Carlos, the one other "person of color" who showed up to tryouts, cocky and well-muscled and joking, telling me, *I don't care what these assholes say, man. This Salvadoran can row.*

I guess it could be all right if we do it together.

I'm not doing crew. Not now. Not without him.

Maybe I'll do this play. Why not, right?

I have absolutely nothing to lose.

"Thanks, Mom," I say, and she gives me one of those looks I'm too familiar with these days, all *what am I going to do with you* and *how can I help* and *talk to me talk to me talk to me.*

But I'm not talking.

I spend the week before school starts killing time and flip-ping channels, hiding out in the air-conditioning and being bored. Just when I'm starting to think I'm going to have to blow up the TV to keep myself entertained, my cell buzzes on the coffee table.

"Damon, yo," a voice on the other end of the line says. "What you up to today, man?"

"Nothin' much, Prague," I say, shifting my phone from one ear to the other. "It's early."

Prague is my cousin. He lives nearby and goes to Hamilton—one of the best public schools in the city, I've been told, repeatedly, by my mom—though in a place where half the students in the public schools don't make it to graduation day, that's not saying a whole hell of a lot. Prague's real name is Samuel, but everybody calls him Prague. I don't know why. Prague probably thinks the name makes him sound pretty gangsta for a guy whose mother is a lawyer and whose dad is a civil engineer. Does he even know it's a city in Europe known for its castles and fancy clocks?

"Well, later it'll be hot as hell, man. You wanna come hang out? We down around Hamilton chillin', playing ball."

"I don't play basketball," I say.

"Come down anyway. You can just chill, whatever."

Dammit. It's not like I got anything better to do.

"All right, cool," I say, smothering a sigh.

I take my time getting to Hamilton, meandering down side streets and circling around and doubling back. On Wisconsin Avenue, I wander past a restaurant I've never seen before called Gary's. It looks like a typical diner, a little run-down, kinda scrappy. Might be worth checking out later. All the restaurants in this neighborhood tend toward the high-end or fast food with nothing in between. I miss my old neighborhood in Shepherd Park—there were diner-type places where I could hang out without people hovering over me all the time trying to refill my water glass or switch out my old fork for a new one. I guess Tenleytown is an upgrade, in a way, but it doesn't feel like it. It just feels less like home.

I watch as people stream in and out, grabbing coffee and a donut or, if they're feeling fancy, a croissant, stuffing copies of the *Washington Post* under their arms as they head toward the Metro and another day of paper pushing and number crunching.

At Hamilton I find Prague and his buddies engaged in a fast-moving pickup game. They're all shirtless and sweating, bodies contorting around each other as they reach and strain and push and shove. I snap a couple shots on Carlos's camera. Prague executes an impressive three-pointer and does a little victory dance, rolling his shoulders. I raise my hand in a wave.

"Damon Lewis!" Prague exclaims, jogging over and slapping me on the back. "Where you been, man?"

"Around," I say. "You know."

"No, I don't know," Prague says. "Hey, J, you wanna let Damon play guard for a bit? I know you tired, man, you look like you about to fall over."

A tall, skinny guy wearing a bandanna and a permanent scowl crosses his arms. "Bullshit, I'm fine."

"I don't want to play—" I start to say.

"Aw, c'mon, man, everybody wants to play," Prague says.

"Seriously," I say. "Prague, I'm cool just hanging out."

Prague's eyes travel over me like he's cataloging me. He takes in the camera bag slung over my shoulder. "You messin' around with that camera, I see."

I shrug.

"You like to watch, huh?" Prague says, a bit of a sneer turning up one corner of his mouth.

I don't know why he's got to make it sound so dirty. I want to punch him in his smug face.

Prague's a good-looking guy, has his mother's dark, almond-shaped eyes and father's espresso skin, and he knows it, likes to carry himself like he's hot shit. I remember when we were kids and would spend Christmases together. Prague would always steal stuff from my stocking, then make fun of me if I started crying.

Prague holds my gaze for a long, uncomfortable moment, then looks away.

I only stay for about half an hour before I get bored with their never-ending stream of bullshit banter and insults. I stand and raise my hand to wave at Prague.

"You going, man?" Prague says, breathless from exertion.

"Yeah," I say.

I got no reason to stay.

I walk back the way I came, crossing Wisconsin, inhaling the combo of concrete and traffic and grease. Sunny, hot air caresses my face and hands, but I can feel fall coming like an old man feels rain in his bad knee—inevitable, painful, new and yet the same thing all over again.

Gary's looks busy, teeming with people. I push my way inside. Retired men with silver-speckled hair sit in corner booths or at the counter, stirring coffee and muttering to each other, complaining about the cracks in the vinyl seats or the lack of good biscuits. The walls are covered with framed old photos: Frank Sinatra and Marlon Brando and Greta Garbo and Marilyn Monroe, plus vintage advertisements for Marlboro cigarettes and Hershey's bars and brands of detergent they don't make anymore.

There are even a few photos of naked ladies, the kind of old-school porn they used to put on the backs of playing cards made for sailors and soldiers. I resist the urge to sit and stare at those pictures, hypnotized by the women's breasts. I'm amazed that people can eat around pictures like that, these strangers so naked and vulnerable up there on the wall baring it all like it's nothing.

A large pregnant woman introduces herself as "Dahlia, honey," and tells me someone will be right with me. I sprawl out on the padded diner seat, take out my copy of *Othello* and read through act 1 again. I've read the play four times in the last week. Every time I do, it seems more complicated and strange. I should understand Othello better now—husband, soldier, leader, murderer!—but I don't.

Why are you so stupid, man? Why do you believe everybody's lies?

"Hello, welcome to Gary's," a voice jerks me out of my reverie.

I look up and see a girl about my age fumbling in her apron for a notepad. Her hair is red-streaked and falls in her face.

"Hi," I say. "How are—"

I stop breathing.

She can't be the same girl. That's crazy. People say this is a small city, but that's just ridiculous.

She looks up then, pad in hand, and our eyes meet.

"I know you," she says, her eyes widening. "You're that guy—"

"I'm not stalking you, I swear," I blurt out.

Dumbass. Stupid, stupid, stupid.

"Good to know," she says. "So what the hell *are* you doing, then?"

"I'm just getting some coffee," I say. "I didn't know you worked here, I—"

"Breathe, dude," she says, mouth quirking at one corner. "I'm not going to call the cops or anything. I believe you."

"Well, good," I say. "I'm glad."

She looks at me like she's trying to figure me out. She glances around, as if she's trying to see if anyone's watching, then slides into the booth across from me.

"You want to talk to me about what happened in the park?" she asks. "You kind of freaked me out, you know."

I exhale and look down at my hands.

"I moved here not that long ago," I say. "I've been wandering around a lot. I ended up in the park and I saw you—"

I don't tell her about the tree, about that spot. About how no matter where I walk, I always end up back there again.

"And you decided to save me from myself?" the girl says. She sounds amused. At least she doesn't seem mad.

"You seemed really upset," I say, and finally meet her eyes again.

You looked like he did when—

"I *was* really upset," the girl says, and her eyes flicker dark. "That's kind of why I was there. Alone. Crying."

"I'm sorry if I—"

"No, hey, look," the girl says, her face softening. "I'm being hard on you. What you did was sweet. It was. I was just caught off guard. You know—alone, in the middle of the park, nobody around—"

"I didn't mean to scare you," I say. "I really didn't."

"We haven't even been formally introduced," she says, and holds out her hand. "I'm Melanie."

"I'm Damon," I say, and take her hand and squeeze it.

"Nice to officially meet you, Damon," Melanie says. "Where'd you come from? I mean, what school—"

"Gate Prep," I say. "Over in Potomac?"

"No shit," she says, lifting an eyebrow. "You still go there, or . . ."

"No, starting at Hamilton soon," I say.

"That's where I go," she says. "Hamilton's going to be . . . different from Gate."

"I hope so," I say. "Gate was—I mean. It's—"

"It's Gate Prep," she says, wrinkling her nose. "It's okay, I understand."

You don't understand, I think. *But it's nice of you to try.*

"The awesome thing about D.C. public schools," she says, "is we only rank, like, forty-ninth in the nation!"

"There's always Alabama," I say, and she smiles.

"Ah, Alabama," she says. "Always there to save us from ourselves."

I find myself smiling too. We lock eyes for a moment, and the air feels different: charged.

Then she blinks and looks away.

"Shit, I actually work here. Even if my dad owns the place, I've still got to hustle," she says, patting the pad of paper in her pocket. She slips out of the booth. "Can I get you anything?"

"Coffee would be great," I say. "Just black."

"Be right back," she says.

"Thanks," I say, and then she turns and is gone.

While she's away, I riffle through my bag, locating the folder containing my most recent prints. I lift it out and open it on the table. There she is: sitting on the ground in front of that tree, eyes lifted to the sky, red hair falling in her face, eyeliner streaks on her cheeks like scars.

I realize I still have no idea why she was crying. Now it's another one of those questions there will never be the right moment to ask.

I hear the clatter of dishware as Melanie approaches, and hastily slide the photograph under the pile so it's on the bottom.

"Who's that?" Melanie asks as she places the cup of coffee on the table in front of me.

I glance down, and my chest tightens. Carlos is staring back at me, head tilted back, smiling wide and giddy. We were watching a soccer game on ESPN when I snapped it. I borrowed Carlos's camera to do it, and Carlos was so caught up in the game, he didn't even notice.

"Oh," I say. I feel breathless. "A friend of mine. Carlos."

"Cute," Melanie says, and smiles. "That's a good photo. You take it?"

I nod.

Carlos is smiling wide, showing his slightly crooked front teeth, and he looks completely relaxed. Like he's so happy in that moment, there's nowhere else he'd rather be.

"That is an amazing picture," she says. "He seems like he'd be a really cool guy."

My hand twitches against the tabletop.

"Was," I say, and my voice is almost swallowed up by the buzz of the restaurant. "He was a really cool guy."

I reach out as if to take the photo back, but then retract my hand.

"Keep it," I say.

"What?" she says, her eyes going wide.

"Keep it," I repeat. I'm a metronome.

"Wait—" she starts to say.

"Keep it, I'm cool," I say, but on every level I'm lying, I'm lying, I'm lying.

I slide the photo across the table and Melanie takes it, scraping its surface with her black-polished nails. Her face changes as she stares at the photo, pupils narrowing, mouth relaxing into a smile.

Seeing her smile like that makes me want to snap another photo of her, to freeze that moment in time before it's gone.

He seems like he'd be a really cool guy.

Was. He was a really cool guy.

Was.

Was.

Was.

What would Carlos have thought about Melanie? He might've made some rude comments about Melanie's fire-engine dye job and piercings and ripped-up clothes, but he probably would've thought she was sassy and funny too.

She's geeky just like you, man. Go for it.

Go for it.

Melanie

I watched you fade, your skin turning the color of dirty
    dishwater. Your hair fell out and you wore wigs,
    different wigs every day, sometimes, dirty blond like
    your real hair, or dark brown and curly, or even
    blue or purple on the days you were feeling better,
    more like yourself, more like Dana Ellis: the artist
    and the work of art.
I knew you were going to laugh on the rainbow hair days,
    that we'd joke around and pretend to be rock stars,
    members of an all-girl punk band with stage names
    like Sally Vicious and Precious Pain. What would
    our band have looked like, an Ellis mother-daughter
    combo?
What would we have sounded like?
But there is no rock band, no rainbow hair, no screaming
    crowds.
There is just me, here, now—me and my red-streaked
    hair, somehow never as bright as yours, no matter
    what color it was.
Me and these trees, and you are gone.

CHAPTER TWO

S o what I'm thinking," Tristan says, swinging his legs over the side of the Metro escalator, "is that this year I can go as Marilyn for Halloween, and you can go as Joe DiMaggio."

I blink. Everything is blurry, and I can't see anything.

"Helloooo," Tristan says, waving his hand in front of my face. "You're not even listening to me, Ellis."

He elbows me in the ribs, and we nearly go toppling backward over the wall. When I manage to right myself, I give him a sharp look.

"We could have fallen, idiot."

"But we didn't!"

He pushes black hair out of his eyes and pouts.

"Can I—"

"No," I say.

"Anything at all," he says. "Align your chakras. Cleanse your aura. Retail therapy."

I smile, but it's only barely a twitch of my lips.

"I saw that," he says. "You were almost amused."

"Shut up," I murmur.

"Retail therapy works," he says. "I saw it on *Oprah* once."

"Mmm," I say. "And everything Oprah says is true."

Tristan presses one hand to his chest, feigning offense.

"She is only the best part of my life, okay, so please do not deride her."

"You and middle-aged housewives everywhere," I say. "She's not even on TV anymore, Tristan."

"That doesn't even slightly diminish her influence. If anyone can teach me how to live, it's Oprah," Tristan says. "Plus she has her own network now, silly."

I stay silent.

His sharp blue eyes flick across my face, and he reaches for my hand. "We should go somewhere."

Tristan is the type of friend who will sit and stay by my side and be quiet and not bother me, but he must know this isn't healthy—the lingering, the being still.

The first phone call I made the day my mother died was to Tristan. He picked up on the first ring.

Oh my God, Tristan said. *Thank you for calling. I am like two seconds away from killing my father.*

Tristan— I whispered.

He is the biggest jerk, I swear, Tristan trundled on. *Are there times when it's considered justifiable homicide just because someone is such a d—*

Tristan, I said, louder. *My mother died.*

The phone went silent for a moment, and I heard Tristan's breathing stutter. It scared me that Tristan wasn't talking. I could count on one hand the number of times Tristan had been at a loss for words.

I'm such an idiot, he said finally. *I am so, so sorry, Melly.*

Everyone always apologizes, like it's their fault.

It's not your fault, I said.

I'll come over right now, he said.

You don't have to—

Yes, I do.

Tristan came over and sat with me for hours, stroking his fingers through my hair as I curled my hands into fists, then opened them, finger by finger, as if I expected to see something different on my palms each time I did it.

Now he leads me down Connecticut Avenue, man on a mission: past the bead store (*Beadazzled!*, the storefront proclaims) and a liquor store and Ann Taylor Loft, past Kramerbooks and a closet-sized art gallery. We grab some coffee at Starbucks and go sit in the Circle itself on one of the benches not currently occupied by homeless people or teenagers making out.

I like Dupont Circle. I like the mixture of law firms and posh boutiques and indie record shops and sex toy stores and ridiculous themed bars and overpriced hipster restaurants. I like perching on the giant gaudy marble fountain in the center of the Circle and watching the boys sidle past in tight jeans and Burberry scarves and eyeliner. On a summer Saturday Dupont is lively and crowded with people shopping and hanging out and eating and sweating.

I've seen all of this so many times.

"Sometimes I can't wait to get out of here," I sigh.

"You want to come to New York with me?"

I smile. "Sure."

"Sounds like a plan. So how are we going to make the

million dollars it takes to live in Manhattan these days?"

"I was thinking a little drug dealing and whoring," I say.

"That's my girl," Tristan says, patting me on the shoulder. "Always the one with the ideas."

When I go silent, Tristan nudges me with his shoulder as if to say, *Stay with me now.*

"So my dad is crazy," he says. "Like, certifiably insane."

"This is news?" I ask.

"Danny wanted to go fishing, right," he says, "and I was like, 'No, I don't want to go fishing, it's boring and gross,' and my dad goes—I'm not joking, Mel—he goes, 'Man up, Tristan. Stop being such a pansy.'"

"Nice," I say. "Sensitive!"

"I don't even hate the outdoors. I hate *fishing.* And yet I spent several days on our so-called vacation fishing with my brothers, which, by the way, is really boring and gross. And I smelled like fish even after I showered, which made me want to eviscerate something that is not a fish, because seriously—"

"Tristan," I say.

He shuts up instantly and takes my hand.

"Tell me, darling."

"Tomorrow school starts," I say. "Can you make me a promise?"

"Anything."

"Can you promise me," I whisper, "that this year will be better than this summer was?"

I blink and for a moment I see Damon, hunched over

25

in the booth at the diner, pretty hands curled around his folder of photos. I see Damon's smile, wide straight teeth and dimples. It was only there for a second, but it was so beautiful when it was.

His eyes were so green.

"Damn right it will be," Tristan says.

I walk home alone after parting from Tristan at the Tenleytown Metro. Billie Holiday coos through my iPod earphones: *ain't nobody's business if I do.*

The air is starting to cool off, D.C.'s brutal humidity breaking. I wander out into my backyard, settle onto the bottom porch step and watch the sun sink slowly out of view, painting the sky golden and pink, eating away the blue.

When I was fourteen we had a party for my mom's forty-fifth birthday. The party was huge and noisy, overflowing into the yard and onto the porch, people perched on every available surface, drinking and eating and laughing and dancing. My dad closed down the restaurant for the night so everyone could come: Macho and Janine and Dahlia and Andrea and all the cooks on the line, José and Rudy and Isaiah. Some of my mom's fellow teachers and a few of her former students showed up, and nearly all her friends made appearances too.

Mom was in top form, dancing around the kitchen with Macho. She was channeling Marlene Dietrich in elegant dress pants with flared legs, a white button-down shirt with the collar open, thin black tie hanging loose around her neck and a black fedora tipped over her brow. She and Macho attempted some kind of tipsy salsa, feet stuttering on linoleum to the syncopated beat. Occasionally she would lean too far to one side and Macho would catch her, keeping her upright, saying, *All right, Dana, don't hurt yourself, darlin'.*

Dad stood in one corner of the kitchen and watched, a smile nudging at his lips, his eyes blurry from liquor and happiness. I watched Dad watch Mom and thought: *He loves her. That's what love looks like.*

Late that night after the last guests had left, Mom lurched up the stairs, drunk but cheerful. She stumbled over a pile of laundry in one corner of the hallway and nearly went sprawling. This time I reached out and helped steady her with one arm. Mom looked down at me, gratitude in her eyes, and smiled wide.

Oh, baby, you shouldn't see me like this, she said. *I'm a mess.*

You look beautiful tonight, Mom, I said, and it was true; with her cheeks all rosy and eyes bright and blond hair falling in waves around her face, she looked gorgeous, alive and amazing. She looked how I wanted to look, like the kind of person who could hold the attention of a room full of people, who could dance badly around a kitchen and laugh and make people laugh with her. My mom brought warmth wherever she went like some kind of human fireplace.

Thank you, sweetheart, she said, pressing one hand to my cheek and smoothing her thumb over my cheekbone. *You're the most beautiful, you know.*

I shook my head no, but she forced me to look up, hand under her chin, and with her eyes shining she said, *Mel, you are, don't ever let anybody tell you different.*

People say strange things when they're drunk. My mom would never have said something like that sober, I'm pretty sure. Not because she didn't mean it, but because it never would have occurred to her. She never seemed to do it on purpose, but she was always the star of the show, the most beautiful, a magnet for the spotlight. This made the rest of us the supporting players, not just on her birthday, but every day.

How could I ever be the most beautiful when she was the sun and I was the moon, pale and only seen because of her reflected light?

And what does that make me now, with her gone?

You're not supposed to think these things about dead people, though, are you? Dead people are supposed to be perfect. Perfect and gone.

That night my dad was in charge of wrangling her.

I best get this woman to bed, he said, appearing at the top of the staircase. He wrapped his arms around Mom's waist and yanked her backward, making her squeal as he tugged her into their bedroom and tossed her down on the bed. They were like little kids, giggling and teasing and tickling each other, and then Dad kicked their door closed.

Suddenly it was too quiet in the hallway. I felt itchy. I padded into my bedroom, went to my bed and sat down on top of the quilt, flicked on the radio and listened to the

DJ on WPGC 95.5 dedicate sultry R&B songs to lovers. I lay on my bed, still in all my clothes, and stared up at the ceiling. The songs melted one into the next, steady rhythm ticking away like a metronome. Soon the voices all sounded the same. Outside my window it started to rain and a chill seeped through the wire mesh screen window. I wrapped my arms around myself and lay still, so still, impossibly still.

Alone, I thought. *This is what alone feels like.*

When my mom got so sick she lost her hair from the chemo and became pale and thin, there were no more parties. She stopped seeing her casual friends and didn't go out hardly at all. With her hair all gone and her skin the color of wax paper and her shaking hands and bloodshot eyes, she wore her secret on the outside now.

I began bringing her ice cream from a neighborhood place we'd discovered together, packaged in their plain white pint cartons with simple black-and-white printed labels: Cookies & Cream. Mint Chocolate Chip. Chocolate. Mango. Coconut. We'd sit on her bed and eat straight out of the container, spoonful by spoonful, until one day she told me she couldn't, that her stomach couldn't handle it. Later I would learn that she hadn't been able to taste for weeks, that the chemo had taken that away from her too.

And then the cancer took her away, period.

My mother wore top hats just for the hell of it, knew how to curse in twelve languages, took a class in tarot card reading on a whim and spent days offering to read the fortunes of everyone she met. She was crazy and unpredictable. *Your mom*, people would say to me, *is such a character. She's fabulous. Unique. Gorgeous.* Sometimes they would look at me skeptically and say, *You've got her eyes*, like they were trying to figure out what I possibly could have inherited from her. Not her charm, or her talent, or her vibrant personality, no. But I had her eyes, my genetic consolation prize.

My mom was so wild, in fact, that I'd always figured she'd be offed in a duel at dawn, or in a freak bungee-jumping accident, or beheaded by a low-flying hot-air balloon.

Cancer? Really?

But death doesn't make sense, does it?

God, just stop. Why can't I make it stop?

My stomach rumbles. It's dark now, and cooler—nearly 8:00 p.m., my watch says. I get up and go inside, wondering why Dad hasn't called me in for dinner. The rare times he's home for dinner, he's usually a fascist about when we eat. It's strange he's not in the kitchen or upstairs.

"Daddy?" I call down the basement steps.

I can see light emanating from below, but no sign of him.

"I'll be up in a minute, sweetheart," comes his voice, low and strained.

I hop down a few steps. I can see the basement more clearly now, crowded with canvases and boxes containing jars of paint and brushes and palettes, all the tools of an artist. Mom's studio lies disassembled here, exploded with no structure or system to it. It's not unlike when she was still using it, except now it's packed away in the dark rather than laid out upstairs in her sunny office off the living room.

Dad began moving stuff downstairs a few weeks before she died. That was when I knew she wasn't coming back from the hospital.

"Are you okay?" I ask.

At the reception after the funeral I'd found my father in the kitchen, making toast.

Dad, I'd said, *what the hell are you doing?*

He looked up at me with bleary eyes. They were dark brown and red at the corners. Bread popped out of the toaster. He looked at it like he didn't know what it was.

There are people out there, he said.

Yeah . . . I prompted.

She's not here, he said.

I thought, *Oh, great, now Mom's gone and Dad's lost his mind.*

Dad, are you okay? I asked, and the moment I said it I regretted it, because of course he was not okay. There was no reason he should be. He'd just buried his wife.

He blinked, then wordlessly handed me a piece of toast. I took it and we chewed in silence, the toast dry and crusty and sandpapery and tasteless. He wrapped one arm around my shoulders, squeezing.

I trip down the rest of the stairs to find my father sitting in a broken wooden chair, running his fingers over a large canvas. In the low light I can make out the swirled colors of a figure, abstract but oddly familiar.

"She gave this to me," he says softly, "on our one-year anniversary. Seventeen years ago."

I flick on the light so I can see. The figure is my dad—visible now—hunched over a stove, cooking. Steam rises in white clouds from the pan, and the flames glow orange fanned out around the burner. His hair is a mass of curls, mostly gone now as he approaches middle age, and he's holding one hand above the pan, sprinkling some powdery substance into it.

"She knew before I did," my father whispers. "She knew what I was meant to do even when I thought, *Oh, be an accountant, that's practical, everyone needs an accountant—*"

He stops, rubbing a palm across his face. I let one hand fall to his shoulder, wanting him to feel me there, close.

"Everyone needs food too, Dad," I whisper.

Laughter bubbles out of his throat, a surprise.

"That is a good point, Melly."

He presses his hand against the canvas over the image of his own face, spreading out his fingers. In between the Vs I can see snatches of color, slivers that don't make sense, color without context.

Damon, boy with the green eyes, standing between the trees—

Who are you?

My brain is such a fog.

"I'm sorry," he says.

Everybody apologizes.

"Sorry for what?" I say.

"I'm sorry I couldn't—"

He stops. I get it. *Save her. Keep her here. Fix her. Sorry*

32

I didn't see that she was sick. Sorry I didn't know until it was too late.

But there are things we can't prepare for, things we don't see.

"Don't be sorry," I say.

Chipping paint, red brick and an underlying aroma of asbestos. Mmm. Welcome back to school, D.C. public-style.

I adjust my bra strap and press my way through the metal detectors. The lockers look pristine and graffiti free. They're only this way during the first few weeks, chartreuse paint glaring and awful but still unblemished. Outside the auditorium is the same display of photos of our sports teams that I'm pretty sure has been there since the building was erected. The photos themselves are universally boring, all depicting past athletes posed to look heroic and fit in uniforms that are almost comically dated at this point. I guess the display remains there to remind us all that sports are great, even as the photos grow increasingly yellow with age.

The hallways hum with the collected energy of fifteen hundred teenagers steeped in a potent hormonal infusion, gabbing about the swampy D.C. August heat and their part-time jobs from hell and who got a new car, new house, new boyfriend or new clothes this summer.

My summer involved waiting tables and lots of bad late-night TV and indie rock played loudly through crackling speakers. There were also endless hospital visits and terrible sludgy cafeteria pudding and many sleepless nights. My mom died, and no one knows that but the one friend I told. No one else cares.

It's amazing how high school works—people spend so much time gossiping, but know so little about each other's lives. My classmates are not so much ships passing in the night as they are bumper cars, constantly crashing into each other but never connecting, never taking the time to see beyond the collision.

"Melly!" Tristan grasps me around the waist and lifts, spinning me in a tight circle.

Nobody is immune to Tristan's hugs. They're like cinnamon toast, good any time of day or night.

Tristan's grinning huge and toothy, braces glinting and blue eyes shining. His hair is dark and messy and falls over his face like rain.

"Happy to see me?" he says.

I sigh and give in, letting him hug me close; he presses his face into my hair. He smells like green tea. God, only Tristan would come to school smelling like a Japanese beverage. I love him.

The bell rings, shrieking and loud. When we separate Tristan makes a face, twisting one hand through his hair. It peaks in front like soft-serve ice cream.

"I have to go see a guy about a thing at lunch," Tristan says. "When will we meet again, my darling?"

"Is this a legal thing? Who is this guy?"

Tristan arches an eyebrow but says nothing.

"After school? You don't have play practice yet, do you?"

Tristan laughs. "Maybe I'll try something else this year. Maybe . . . basketball."

I snort. "Mmm-hmm. Magic eight ball says, 'Not likely.'"

Tristan flips me off good-naturedly. I blow him a kiss.

Bio happens, then English, then study hall. My classes are uneventful and uninteresting, and I spend most of bio making tiny origami birds out of pieces of my schedule. I applaud my own productivity.

After school I settle down under a tree and watch my fellow students stream out of the building like noxious gas, off to pollute the rest of the world for the evening. Say what you will about the American education system, but at least it contains my worthless generation for eight hours a day. I like to think of school as not so much a prison as a mental hospital, a holding cell for those plagued with the unfortunate pathology known as adolescence.

"Melly!" Tristan collapses onto the ground next to me, pulling me into a tight embrace. "It's been years."

"Jesus, Tristan," I say, coughing. "Leave some oxygen in my lungs, please. I need it for respiration and, y'know, not dying."

Tristan's all sunny smiles when he lets me go.

"Oh my God, okay, so I was talking to Mr. Granger, right," Tristan says, "and he thinks I might be right about that thing about the Illuminati—"

I try to pay attention to Tristan's rambling account of how the Catholic Church was possibly allied with some crazy evil secret society, but I tune him out after the first thirty seconds and watch the procession of human traffic instead. It's a never-ending stream of jeans, T-shirts and sneakers, disrupted occasionally by random piercings, ugly possibly fake tattoos or ill-advised dye jobs.

But then my eyes catch and hold.

Damon.

I'd wondered when I would see him.

At the restaurant, I didn't get a chance to check him out for real. I take a moment to just look. He's tall, lanky, wearing a black T-shirt and baggy jeans over beat-up Pumas. His skin's the color of a latte, with dark, wiry hair and eyes so green, they'd make Kermit jealous. Serious cheekbones too, high and angled and sharp. He's got a camera case slung over one shoulder. He's leaning against a wall in front of the school, chatting with some guys on the basketball team. He holds up one long-fingered hand and forms it into the shape of a gun, pointing it at one of his laughing friends.

I watch as he talks to one of the ballers. At first they seem to be joking around, but then Damon shrugs off the other boy and turns away. He slides down the wall into a crouch and pulls a camera out of his bag. He raises it to look through the viewfinder and his fingers tighten around the lens, adjusting.

Is he looking at me?

". . . and that's how they killed Jimmy Hoffa! It's so totally fascinating, Melly . . . Melanie?"

Tristan has to nearly throttle my arm to recover my

attention. I blink and turn away, focusing on Tristan's face.

"You all right, Mel?" Tristan cocks an eyebrow.

"M'good," I mutter, brushing strands of my hair out of my eyes. "But I got homework, so I'll catch you later."

"Bye, babe," Tristan says, then hops up and gives me yet another hug. He feels warm and smells sweet. *We'll talk about this later, missy,* his eyes are saying, but it's more of a promise than a threat.

At home, safely ensconced in my room, I slip a Nina Simone CD into my stereo, curl into a ball and listen to her wail about the world's woes. But when I close my eyes, I think of Damon: Damon who drinks black coffee and has green eyes, Damon who *goes to my school.* When he told me he was starting at Hamilton, I didn't think about what that really meant.

I make up a life for him. Maybe he's the only child of two very attractive parents. He plays basketball and thinks *Sports Illustrated* is great journalism. He's never read a poem in his life. He's polite, but not very smart. He only likes action movies, watching people get blown up. On weekends he goes out with his friends and they drink and knock over trash cans and laugh like it's the funniest thing in the world.

But that doesn't seem right.

You never give boys a chance, Melly, my mom used to say. She'd be sitting in the kitchen with her paint-stained fingers wrapped round a cup of coffee, looking at me through the thin, wire-rimmed glasses that were sliding down her nose.

I give them a chance, I'd say.

Girls either, she'd say.

Maybe that was fair. It'd been me and Tristan forever, bonded by our mutual love of Spider-Man coloring books in the first grade, but I haven't had a really good girlfriend for years. I know exactly when I stopped trying to make them: middle school. That's when everyone got mean, when the jokes turned cruel and the insults got personal. My clothes were never stylish enough. My hair was never cute enough. *Hey, Melanie, 1974 called and it wants your flared jeans back,* Sophie Angelino said to me once. It felt like the whole room laughed.

Who wants friends like that?

My mom couldn't possibly understand, because I wasn't like her: everybody's buddy, so charming and easy and pretty. I didn't make instant connections with people. I didn't fit in. I couldn't just flirt and toss my hair and flutter my eyelashes and make the boys come to me. Boys didn't look at me that way. They didn't look at me at all.

Sometimes I wondered if that was because there was nothing to look at.

I'd give them a chance, I'd think, *if they'd give me one.*

I riffle through my purse to find the photo Damon gave me of Carlos. It's beautiful. I don't even know this kid and every time I look at it I want to smile.

Maybe that was Damon's way of giving me a chance. Letting me in.

What is up with that camera? It seems like his constant

companion. I feel like there's a story there, and I want to know it.

Damon could have walked away when he saw me crying in those woods. That's what most other people would have done. That's the kind of world we live in, filled with people looking the other way.

But Damon cared. He'd wanted to help.

That means something.

Saturday, my dad tells me Grandma Agnes wants me to visit.

I am not excited about this.

I don't dislike Grandma Agnes, exactly. She's my mom's mother, and my only living grandparent. My dad's parents died when I was little, so I never got to know them very well, and my mom's father died before I was born.

Still, Grandma Agnes and I have never exactly been close—she used to come to my mom's shows and to dinner sometimes, but it always seemed like there was this impossible distance between her and my mom, like they were just too different to connect in any real way. My mom never talked about it, but I got the sense that Grandma Agnes never quite understood why my mom wanted to be an artist.

Once at Thanksgiving I overheard them talking in the hallway, Grandma Agnes saying in that tone that didn't allow for any dispute: *Teaching is noble, Dana, but with Gary leaving accounting for the restaurant, you're always struggling. You're so sharp, you could—*

Oh my God, Mom, I heard my mother say. *Just give it a rest.*

But if you did something practical—

My mom didn't reply. She just walked away, passing me in the hallway but saying nothing, like she didn't even see me.

That was the thing about my mom: To understand her, you had to understand her as an artist. It was so much a part of her, so much of what she loved and what she did and how she saw the world. She did art because she had to, because it was in her veins. Not just because she didn't want to stop, but because she couldn't.

These days Grandma Agnes is a little crazy, but that's not her fault. She's eighty years old, after all. At a certain age you're allowed to get rid of all your filters and say whatever comes into your head with no regard for people's feelings, and it's not like she was ever that filtered to begin with.

"Please don't argue with me about this," my dad says. "Just go."

"Are you not even going to come with?" I ask, and he shakes his head.

Great. He's sending me in like a sacrificial lamb.

"That's not fair—"

"Melly," he says, and his whole body seems to deflate, "she wants to see you. I know this isn't what you want to be doing with your Saturday, but she's your grandmother and she loves you. Please just spend this one afternoon with her, okay?"

Thus in spite of my total lack of motivation to go, I end up spending my Saturday afternoon over at my grandmother's in her warm, stuffy box of an apartment. The whole place is outfitted in various floral prints—floral couch, floral curtains, floral wallpaper, paintings of flowers on the walls. It is a bouquet of an apartment. You would think having so many floral patterns would make it cheerful, but it smells musty and stale and she keeps all the shades closed all the time, so it's dark and gloomy. There are no actual flowers in the apartment.

She serves me a tuna fish sandwich. She's wearing a sweater with giraffes on it, which is pretty much the way Grandma Agnes rolls.

"I wanted to see how you're holding up," she says.

I take a tentative bite of my sandwich. Grandma Agnes is not known for her culinary expertise, but this tastes like it probably won't kill me.

"I'm okay," I say.

She looks at me skeptically.

"You look tired," she says. "Are you sleeping?"

I shrug.

She sighs.

"What is all this, Melanie?" she says, gesturing to what seems to be all of me.

"What?" I say.

"All of this," she says. "A few months ago you were perfectly normal. Now you've got that hair, and all the jewelry in strange places, and you wear these clothes that look like they've been run over by a car."

Today I'm wearing my less ripped-up jeans and a Smiths

T-shirt I found in a thrift store a few weeks ago. This is about as presentable as I get these days.

"This is what I want to wear," I say.

I think of the day I first dyed my hair red. It was the same day my mom had gone in for her last round of chemo. The doctors hadn't said it was the last round, but the treatment was pretty much useless at that point—the cancer was spreading and none of the previous rounds had worked. *This is my Hail Mary pass*, my mom said, and shot me a smile that was jagged at the edges. I spent several hours sitting outside the bathroom door, listening to her throw up. Eventually I got her into bed and she fell asleep. I went upstairs and used the dye Tristan and I bought for Halloween last year to put in scarlet streaks. When I came downstairs she was awake. She looked at me and reached out and ran her hands through my hair. It looked so red against her fingers, her skin as white as I'd ever seen it.

I like it, she said. *You know I used to have my hair like that when I was your age.*

Really? I said. *Was that during your punk rock phase?*

I hear air quotes in your voice, she said. *I resent those air quotes.*

I would never, I said.

I will have you know, she said, somehow mustering superiority even in her exhausted state, *that I have always been and will always be punk rock.*

Mmm-hmm, I said.

It's a state of mind, not a state of hair.

42

Mom, I said. *A state of hair?*

She made a dramatic motion with her hand. *Now give me that wig with the green streaks so we can match.*

During the last few months, my mom got paler and paler until she seemed like she was literally fading away, being erased off the page by an unforgiving piece of pink rubber. She faded and weakened and waned. The more she changed, the more I did. Pierced my ears, one hole for every day I came home to find her on her knees throwing up in the bathroom, body wracked with dry heaves. Ripped up my jeans until they were as shredded as my nerves. Bought T-shirts bearing the vulgar names of bands I'd never listened to under the guise of rebelling against the status quo. Watched the dirt collect under my fingernails and wondered what grave I was trying to climb out of.

Suddenly I was the sun: glaring, burning, too bright to look at directly. My mom was the moon: waning, waning crescent, gone.

"Is this some kind of teenage thing?" Grandma Agnes says. "I know sometimes teenagers want to rebel, but you were always so sensible."

Sensible. Yes, that was me. Sensible, practical, quiet. Boring, boring, boring.

"It's not a rebellion," I say.

"Is this about your mother?" Grandma Agnes says.

That same day in the park that I met Damon, I sat there in the spot where we used to go sometimes to draw together and thought: *I'll never be with her here again.* It felt like being stabbed. All those months I watched her die, and yet it never seemed real. Permanent. I was never raised religious, but all of a sudden it made sense why we have so many stories about the afterlife.

How can someone just be gone?

Maybe wearing these clothes and dyeing my hair and wearing jewelry in strange places is stupid. I know it won't bring my mom back. It didn't when she was sick, and it certainly won't now.

But when I dress like this I feel safer, closer to her. More in a punk rock state of mind.

I feel more like I can handle this. More like I can live my life without her.

I can't be quiet Melanie anymore, boring Melanie who slips under the radar, who makes things easier by never asking for anything.

The world is stuck with this Melanie now.

But I don't think this is something that Grandma Agnes will understand.

"It's not about my mom," I say.

DAMON

You always said I was a wuss about talking to girls.
    Big plans, D, you'd say. Big plans and no game.
You were probably right about that.
But what did you know about girls, anyway? All those
    girls you messed around with, and none of them
    ever seemed to mean anything to you.
You never said: This one, man. This time it's for real.
How come I never noticed that?

CHAPTER THREE

So I'm trying out for the play, because why not? If I get a part, it'll get me out of the house, away from my parents. It'll give me something to do. I think I need that: focus.

Before the first round of auditions, I immerse myself in Etta James. She drawls and growls in my earbuds, the melody a slow burn. It always feels like Etta's putting on a private show for me when she sings, voice so intimate and dirty.

I glance around the dimly lit theater, watching people move soundlessly, laughing, shoving each other, gossiping with expressive hand gestures. I narrate a conversation in my head between two girls who are sitting on the edge of the stage in matching dark corduroy miniskirts and knee-high boots, legs dangling.

You don't even know, girl. He is so stupid.

Stupid how?

Stupid like boys always are. Thinking with the wrong head.

I reach for the camera without thinking, hold it up and snap a picture. Neither girl seems to notice; they're too involved in their deep discussion of *who-knows-what* and *who cares.*

A hand drops onto my shoulder. I tense, placing the camera down beside me. One of my earbuds falls out and now Etta's only half-singing to me, the audio unbalanced. A boy with dark hair and light blue eyes is staring down at me and mouthing something. I take out the other earbud and lean forward, cupping my hand around my ear.

"What?" I ask.

"What're you listening to?" the boy asks. "Must be something good. You looked like you were somewhere far away."

I tilt my head. "Have I seen you before?"

The boy smiles, teeth glinting with his shiny metal braces. "I don't know, have you? You know all us white boys look the same."

I find myself smiling back.

"Etta James," I say.

"Ohhh," the boy exhales. "That woman—I get it. She was a goddess. If I were straight and she was alive, I'd totally do Etta James. Maybe anyway. I mean—not the dead part, but you know what I mean."

"Good to know," I say, suppressing a laugh.

"I'm Tristan," the boy says. "I've never seen you before. I'd remember if I had."

Oh man. I think Carlos has used that line before.

"Damon," I say, holding out my hand. Tristan takes it and shakes it, his grip firm.

"So what's a nice boy like you doing in a place like this?" Tristan continues.

"I'm trying out," I say. "For the play."

"Do you mean that in the . . ." Tristan says, then wrinkles

his nose. "Actually, scratch that. I'm so rude, I'm just—you're *very* cute, and—"

"I'm not gay," I say. "I'm not even sure if I'm an actor."

Tristan waves his hand. "Well, none of us knows that. But you are sure you're not . . . ?"

"Yeah," I say. "I'm sure."

"People might think—"

"I don't care what people think," I say.

Tristan looks at me carefully, eyes scanning my face.

"Okay," he says.

There's a clatter at the front of the auditorium. A harried-looking woman appears, wearing an elaborately patterned multicolored scarf and earrings that I am fairly certain are small dogs, gesturing widely with her hands.

"Come, come," she says. "Gather round if you're here for the tryouts!"

I steel myself, already thinking as Othello:

My parts, my title, and my perfect soul shall manifest me rightly.

Tristan is called first. He's confident and comfortable onstage, his articulation and voice projection demonstrating years of theater training. Tristan's more than just well-trained, though; he's *good*. In his hands Cassio gains a complexity I never thought of Cassio possessing, a remarkable feat for a character often written off as a one-dimensional pretty boy who serves as a convenient plot device.

"Reputation, reputation, reputation!" Tristan groans, head in his hands. "O, I have lost my reputation! I have lost the immortal part of myself, and what remains is bestial."

It's then that I realize where I recognize Tristan from. He's Melanie's friend. I saw them together outside school on the first day, talking and laughing. I'd almost taken their picture, but then I'd thought: *No. Not again.*

When I'm called, I feel nothing but relief. Onstage I forget everything but my lines, forget the audience, forget the way my bedroom still feels like a hotel room no matter how I decorate it. I forget I'm the new kid.

I forget Carlos, forget the scar on his upper lip, forget the way he sounded when he laughed or the way he pushed hair out of his eyes when he was being completely truthful and honest.

I'm not even lying, man, Carlos would say. *Sounds fucking crazy, I know, but seriously. Seriously, yeah.*

When I finish, I stride offstage with more confidence than I feel. In the wings I bend over and press my hands into my thighs, exhaling through my mouth in a long *whoosh.*

"You okay?"

I turn to see Tristan. He's watching me with concern, arms crossed over his chest.

"You're everywhere, man," I say, letting out a nervous laugh.

"Get used to it," Tristan says. "I think we're going to be seeing a lot of each other, my friend."

I wipe one hand across my forehead. I feel overheated, though my skin is cool. "Why do you say that?"

"Because you're going to be Othello," Tristan says.

There is no room in his voice for argument.

"Really?" I say.

"Yeah," Tristan says. "She'd have to be crazy not to cast you, man."

I feel my cheeks heat, jamming my hands into my pockets. "I don't know about that."

"Well, I do," Tristan says.

There's a moment of silence. I don't know what to say.

"I didn't mean anything by what I said before, by the way," Tristan says. "I was just messing around."

I can see it, the moment of fear, when Tristan wonders: *Are you going to be like the others?*

"I know," I say, and give Tristan a small smile. "It's cool, man."

After auditions, I head toward the bus, earphones wedged firmly in my ears. A horn blasts so loudly, I hear it above the loud, thumping sounds of Otis Redding. I look up to see Prague leaning out of the passenger seat of a big black truck, shouting something at me.

"Hey, pretty boy!" Prague says. "You want some candy?"

"I'm good, thanks," I say as the truck slows to a stop beside me.

"You need a ride?" Prague asks. "Me and Jackson, we want to give you a ride."

My eyes dart back and forth between Prague and the driver of the truck, the same guy in the bandanna who kept giving me angry looks when I was watching them play ball.

"I can walk," I say.

"Aw, c'mon, cuz," Prague drawls. "Get in the truck."

I figure it's not worth fighting Prague on this, so I pull open the door and get in. Jackson still says nothing, just leans in and turns up the radio a little louder, magnifying the sound of Lil Wayne's obnoxiously detailed description of some woman's ass.

"Why you here so late?" Prague asks, twisting around in his seat to look at me. "We just got done with practice. Coach is fucking crazy, man. He made Jackson run suicides for no reason."

I can see Jackson's hands tighten on the wheel.

Run suicides.

They call them suicides.

Seriously?

"I was auditioning for the play," I say.

Prague's mouth goes slack. "You were . . . what?"

In the driver's seat, Jackson snorts.

"Auditioning for the play," I repeat. "The fall play."

Prague looks stumped. "Really? You don't think that's kind of—"

"—fucking gay?" Jackson finishes. It's the first thing he's contributed to the conversation.

"No, actually," I say. "I don't think it's particularly homosexual that I'm participating in the play."

"All the theater kids are straight-up fags," Jackson states.

"Yeah, D, he's not lying," Prague says.

"Oh, really," I say, leaning forward in my seat. "How do

you know this, Jackson? You spend a lot of time hanging with the theater kids?"

Jackson may be an asshole, but he's not an idiot. He catches the edge in my voice, and he gets what I'm implying.

"You know something, Lewis?" he says, voice low. "You can walk."

"Happy to," I say, and at the next light I get out of the truck without another word.

Carlos was certainly capable of being a macho jerk, but he'd never acted like being into theater was bad or wrong or stupid. Only once did he question my decision to do it, one quiet fall evening a year ago after play practice. We sat together on the comfy couch in my basement, watching some shitty movie starring Adam Sandler or Will Ferrell. Carlos was unusually quiet and distant, curled up with his knees pulled into his chest like he was trying to be as small and compact as possible. Carlos wasn't a big guy to begin with—a little on the short side, broad across the shoulders but nowhere else. He practically disappeared into the cushions. I had asked him what was bothering him earlier, but Carlos brushed me off with a hasty *Nada, hombre, shhh*, and so we just sat silently in a room too small for silences.

I don't know, man, Carlos said suddenly, as if we'd been in the middle of a conversation. *Don't you ever wonder— don't you ever think about what people might say about you being into theater and shit?*

I turned my head to look at Carlos full-on. Carlos was resting his chin on his knees, staring straight ahead.

I thought you didn't give a shit about what people think, I said.

Well, yeah, Carlos said. *But that's me, that ain't you. People like you.*

People like you too.

What is this, you gay for me or some shit? Get off my jock, man, Carlos burst out, glaring at me. *Fuck that, man, and fuck you.*

I was used to Carlos's sudden anger. He'd lash out like a viper, but he was always sorry for it afterward. I could hear his dad whenever he got like that: *Don't pussy out on me, Carlito. Don't be a little pussy.*

If people can't handle me being into theater, then they can't handle being my friends, I said. *I don't need that kind of BS in my life.*

Carlos was quiet for a moment, digging his chin into his kneecap.

I'm not saying I don't get it, Carlos said. *I get why sometimes it's nice to be somebody else for a while.*

I never thought about it, back then—what he meant. Doesn't everybody want to be somebody else sometimes? To escape?

Not the way Carlos did.

Carlos always got it. He always got me.

But sometimes—I guess—I didn't get him at all.

The next morning, I stare at the sheet pasted onto the bulletin board next to the auditorium, the words *Cast List* going fuzzy before my eyes.

"I told you so."

I turn to see Tristan grinning up at me.

"You're so stealthy," I say. "You gotta stop doing that, man. Freaks me out."

"You're always in your own little dream world, that's your problem," Tristan says. "Didn't anyone ever teach you to be aware of your surroundings?"

"Guess not," I say.

"Congratulations," Tristan says. "I knew you'd be Othello."

"Michael Cassio, not too shabby." I nod.

"Yeah, hey, I get to be a shallow douchebag who's sort of in love with a hooker, who doesn't love that?" Tristan says.

"I think that's why it's called 'acting,'" I say.

"Aw, you are too kind," Tristan demurs. "I don't know about the shallow douchebag part, but I can tell you I haven't recently been in love with a hooker."

"Recently?" I raise my eyebrows.

"Not for six months at least."

"Might have to get all method up in here," I say, and Tristan's smile widens.

"Walk with me, Mr. Lewis," Tristan says, and gestures down the hallway.

"Is that weird?" I ask, trailing behind Tristan as we navigate through the sea of bodies. "I mean, playing straight?"

"Not really," Tristan says. "No weirder than anything else. Acting is acting." He hitches his book bag up on his shoulder. "Unfortunately it's probably the role I have the most experience playing, so practice makes perfect, right?"

My chest hurts, like someone reached inside and squeezed.

"Mmm, physics, my favorite," Tristan says as we arrive at the lab. "See you later at practice, O. Can I call you O for short?"

I shrug.

Tristan flutters his eyelashes and curls his hands into the shape of a heart, right at the center of his chest.

I see Prague in the cafeteria at lunch, sitting at a table with all his basketball buddies. He's talking and laughing and making huge, obscene gestures with his hands, probably telling a story about some girl he picked up, then dropped. I watch him for a full minute before Prague glances over. He lifts his hand as if to wave but seems to edit the gesture, never completing it.

Fuck it. I don't need that kind of BS in my life.

At rehearsal I feel overwhelmed by the sheer number of strangers, all of whom seem to know each other intimately. Tristan's nowhere to be found, so I'm forced to make polite, awkward conversation with my fellow actors. One is Lacey Andrews, who's been cast as Desdemona. She's tall and thin and pretty with long, curly blond hair and blue eyes. She tosses her head and her curls bounce around like excited little kids.

"I'm really psyched to get to work with you," she says. "I didn't get to see your audition, but Tristan says you're a major talent."

I feel like I'm at some Hollywood party and Tristan has been acting as my high-powered agent. I realize, suddenly, how this must look—me, the new kid, sauntering into these auditions and taking the lead. If I were one of these kids, I probably wouldn't like me very much.

"Thanks," I say. "I hope I'm all right."

Mrs. McAvoy is late showing up, and in a desperate last-minute move, I dive backstage to escape the small talk. I never know how to answer the stupid questions people ask. Where'd you transfer from? *Somewhere else.* Do you like it here? *Jury's still out.*

I've always been fascinated by backstage: its musty, dusty air, the many ropes and pulleys and mysterious wires. I never know quite what I'm going to find, and I love that. I step over planks of wood and run my hands over scattered sequins and feathers and felt, vestiges of productions past.

Though I'm used to finding the unexpected backstage, I'm still surprised to see Tristan draped all over a tall boy pressed up against one of the rafters, engaged in some pretty serious making out. The other boy is wearing what looks to be a soccer uniform, but that's not doing much to deter Tristan from getting his hand into his shorts.

I try to take my leave without the two of them noticing me, but my foot hits a prop sword, sending it spinning noisily across the floor.

The two boys jump apart like they've been shocked with a cattle prod.

"Oh, hey," I say, lifting my hand in an awkward wave. "My bad. I didn't know you were back here."

"Bryan—" Tristan starts to say, but the boy is already backing away and smoothing out his clothes.

"I'll see you later," Bryan says, averting his eyes. "I gotta go to practice anyway."

Bryan's gone so fast, I wonder for a moment if I hallucinated him. But when I turn back to see Tristan leaning against the wall, face flushed and hair a mess . . . yeah. Not quite.

"Sorry for the cockblock," I say. "Seriously, I didn't—"

"Hey, no worries," Tristan says, attempting to smooth down his hair. "We've got practice too, right? And better you than Mrs. McAvoy." He shudders.

"That is probably true," I say, smiling. "So . . . boyfriend?"

Tristan gives an ambivalent nod of the head as he buttons up his shirt so only a tiny V of undershirt shows. "Ish. I don't know, it's weird, Bryan and I had this whole thing last year that I thought—I guess I thought it was a onetime type of deal? But then I saw him in English and we started chatting and he kept texting me and—" Tristan stops. "It's really stupid and sixth grade, I don't know. I probably shouldn't be talking about it."

"Is it a secret?" I ask.

"Well, it's not like Bryan is out and proud, being Mr. Varsity Soccer." Tristan rolls his eyes. "And hello, neither am I."

I look at Tristan with disbelieving eyes.

"Look, let's just say I like to think of this school as my personal Vegas. What happens here stays here," Tristan says. "My dad's in politics. He works for a Republican senator, for God's sake. He prefers a constant state of denial to the less charming reality."

A bunch of pieces slot into the Tristan jigsaw puzzle. Never judge a person by what you see or don't see.

I feel like I should know that by now.

"Well, okay then. I think we've got rehearsal," I say with a lift of an eyebrow. "So you might want to leave your personal Vegas and come hang with us in Venice."

"This is a true tragedy," Tristan mourns. "After you, sir."

Rehearsal is mostly uneventful. It's just a table read, no blocking yet, and all the sitting still is making me crazy. Shakespeare's words are so powerful that I want to stride around the stage and gesture and exclaim, but I know this is the first step: Learn the language, understand it, then give it dynamic movement and action.

I notice Lacey studying me. It makes me uncomfortable to be under such a microscope, but this too is part of the process. There will only be more eyes on me when I get up on that stage.

After rehearsal I almost run into Prague coming out of the auditorium—he's standing right outside the door. He takes a couple of rapid steps backward and stuffs his hands into the pockets of his baggy jeans, trying to look casual.

"Practice got out a little early," Prague explains. "You want to walk with me?"

"No ride today, huh," I observe.

"Jackson had shit to do. I don't know," Prague says.

I nod. I follow Prague down the hallway and out into the parking lot, Prague's loping stride rhythmic and steady.

"You sure you want to walk with me, man?" I ask. "You know I might be—"

"Hey, I never said that," Prague interrupts. "Was Jackson who said that."

"You agreed with him," I say.

Prague looks down at his shoes, shoulders slumping. "It ain't like that, D, we were just being—"

"Ignorant, right," I say. "Because that makes it better. What're you afraid of, Prague? That you're gonna catch the faggot bug?"

Prague tenses. "Why you always gotta be like that, D? You always act like you better than everybody else."

"I don't—" I say, but then stop.

I feel like I don't know anything anymore.

Prague is silent for a few moments as we walk down Wisconsin. Cars stream by, and Prague's sneakers make high-pitched whines against the sidewalk.

"I heard about your friend," Prague says softly.

I stop in my tracks, hands clenching into fists at my sides.

"You heard what about my friend?"

Prague reaches out and grasps my arm. "Heard your friend . . . I heard you lost a friend, man, and that sucks. You're my cousin, I don't want you to be alone with that."

I will always be alone with that.

"I can make my own friends," I say. "I don't need yours."

Prague's fingers feel tight around my biceps, too tight. He drops his hand from my arm.

"All right then," Prague murmurs. "All right."

We part ways on the next block. I walk toward my house, but when I near my own block I think: *No, not yet.*

I detour into Rock Creek Park, tripping over the uneven ground, pushing aside tree branches as I circumvent the path.

I heard about your friend.

You heard what about my friend?

I settle onto a tree stump and gaze up at the canopy of trees overhead, branches intertwined like tangled yarn, and watch the light disappear until I'm shrouded in darkness.

I close my eyes. I can see it in my mind: my phone on the side table by the couch in my parents' living room, ringing.

My ear itched, my hand wandered, I picked it up. On the other line: Carlos.

He said: *I don't know, man. I don't know.*

You don't know what?

I'm so dizzy, man, he said. *I can't see.*

In movies, scenes like this always end in sirens and flashing lights, the grim parade of a rescue. But it didn't end that way. I was too slow.

Carlos, I said, but all I heard was dead air.

I took the phone and walked down Kalmia, made a left and a right, walked down Georgia Avenue, traced the path I'd taken a thousand times before, and was at Carlos's front door in minutes. No one came when I rang the doorbell. Nobody was home.

I leaned against the door and it cracked open. What the fuck. Carlos never left the front door unlocked. Much of Petworth still wasn't safe enough for unlocked doors. My stomach twisted like rope. I pushed until it gave, walked down the hallway to Carlos's room, ignored the cracked yellow *No Trespassing* sign on the door and shoved my way in.

Carlos's room was so neat: bed made, no clothes on the floor, curtains pulled tight around the windows so even the streetlights didn't penetrate. All the posters were gone, walls blank, cracks in the paint like jagged scars. I will always remember the way the sheets and blankets on Carlos's bed were tucked in, folded under to form hospital corners. Carlos never made his bed. The place looked like a hotel room, clean and tidy and ready for its next occupant. Except—

On the bed was Carlos's camera, black and square and bulky. Next to it perched a cardboard box. I flipped off the lid. Inside were photos, piles and piles of them: Carlos's sisters, his mom, his dad, the Potomac, the monuments, strangers; a child playing in the grass on the Ellipse, uprooting the green by its tender roots and tying the blades into knots; a giant steel sculpture of a flower, metal stamen protruding obscenely from the center; the lonely spinning Smithsonian carousel, flashing colors and intricately carved wooden animals with no one to ride them.

And then there were photos of me—laughing, making

faces, looking somber, dressed up, wearing sweatpants, giving Carlos a mock salute.

Carlos's whole life was in that box. Many lives were in that box.

I don't know why I took it. There was no note, no instructions, nothing that said: *Damon, this is for you.* But I knew. I knew it was for me.

I called my dad on his cell. No answer. I dialed Carlos's number.

The number you have dialed cannot be reached at this time.

I don't know, man.

I jogged home, climbed into my car and drove around for a while, not knowing where to go. Up and down Fourteenth Street, over onto Connecticut, across the bridge into Virginia and back.

A real friend would know. A real friend would sense it. What was it Carlos always used to say? *I feel you. I feel you, man.* But I didn't feel anything, no sixth sense, no aura, just a terrible twist of panic in my gut and my own sweat against the steering wheel. It was beginning to rain.

I called my dad again. This time he picked up.

Damon, where are you? he asked.

I had no idea. There were tight clusters of trees around me. I turned onto a main street and saw a gas station glowing ahead, *OPEN 24 HOURS.*

I'm looking for Carlos, I said.

Damon. Dad sounded disappointed. *It's late.*

Dad, Carlos is in trouble—

He's always in trouble. Let him sort out his own mess.

I wanted to explain, but couldn't. What was I supposed to say? *I think, maybe—*

I'm so dizzy, man. I can't see.

I lost my cell phone signal. Rain slashed across my windshield with karate chop precision. In my mind I could see Carlos bleeding, wrists stained red. Carlos used to talk about stuff like that. I always thought he was kidding.

My jaw hurt from being clenched tight. I called my mom on her cell. She answered, sounding worried: *Baby, it's really coming down out there.*

Mom, I said. *I think Carlos is hurt.*

Hurt how, sweetheart?

My phone buzzed next to my ear. The hairs on my neck stood at attention. I hung up on her, clicked over to call waiting.

D. Carlos's voice sounded faded. *Hey.*

So casual. Carlos was always so fucking casual.

My fingers dug into the scratchy fabric of the car seat. I yanked the steering wheel to the right, parked by the side of the road and watched the rain clean my windows with sheets of water.

Where are you? I asked.

Nowhere. I'm nowhere, man.

Let me come get you, I said. *Tell me where you are, just let me—*

I won't be here when you get here.

My throat felt like it was closing up. *What the hell are you talking about, Carlos? Jesus—*

My phone connection fizzled out again. *Shit,* I hissed. *Shit, fuck, fuck, fuck*—

I called, and called, and called again.

Later the police asked me what Carlos had said to me. Had there been clues?

What kind of question is that? I shouted.

My mother grasped my shoulders as if to hold me back. The detective's eyes widened slightly. He was young, with light hair and blue eyes. He looked at me as if he thought I was going to bite him.

It'd be easier that way, wouldn't it? Just another angry black boy, right? Is that what I am?

There were so many questions afterward, and none of them the right ones. They asked: *Was he depressed? Did something happen in his life that might have prompted him to—? Was he prone—? Did he talk about—? Did he seem—?*

Never: *What was he like?* Never: *Was he a good friend?*

If I squint in the darkness right now I can still see Carlos, leaning against that huge, gnarled tree, smiling.

What the fuck are you so happy about? I would ask.

Carlos would shrug. *I feel better, man. I feel fine.*

What the hell, dude, you just—

Carlos would tilt his head in the way he used to do, like he was trying to see something just out of his sight line. *It was easy.*

Easy?

Yeah. Dying is the easy part.

64

• • •

I shiver. The air has cooled with the setting sun, wind gossiping in the trees: *shhhhhhh.*

Me and Carlos used to sit on the fire escape at Carlos's family's apartment at night and watch people in the street, arguing and flirting and fighting and talking. We would sit there until Carlos's father stopped shouting and stormed out, until his mother stopped crying, until Carlos was ready to go back inside and face everything in there.

But Carlos was never ready to face it, not really. All those shouting matches and insults and tears came raining down on Carlos and seeped under his skin, pooling and weighing him down until he couldn't take it, couldn't be the one holding up his whole world anymore.

That doesn't seem right, though. It doesn't feel like enough of an explanation.

I don't know what could explain this.

I tried to be there, to be the family Carlos needed. I gave him a place to crash when things got hard, took him to movies and concerts and games to distract him, spent many afternoons playing video games. It was no hardship—I loved hanging with Carlos, even when it meant I hardly ever had time to be with anyone else.

I don't know what I'd do— Carlos said once, voice rough, and I squeezed his shoulder, didn't let him finish because I didn't want to hear *without you,* didn't want to consider that possibility.

Now I wake up every morning at the crack of dawn, a reflex from the last two years of early morning crew practices. I'm halfway dressed before I realize I've got nowhere to go and no one to meet me there—no Carlos to harass as he rubs at his eyes and waves me away, mumbling, *I'm tired, fuck you, D, you morning person.*

Sometimes I dial his number on my phone, or check my Facebook expecting to see he's tagged me in some dumb video post about goats, or open up our text thread like I'm going to send him a message. But the last message I sent him was months ago. It said: `dude, you ok?`

He never replied.

Sometimes I'm so angry at Carlos, I want to grasp him by the shoulders and shake him and demand: *Why? Why did you do that?*

But to do that he'd have to be here, close enough for me to touch.

Sometimes I don't believe it.

Sometimes I think: *No way, Carlos would never do that.* It's impossible for him to be dead at seventeen. He was too young, too stupid to die.

There were too many things he hadn't done yet.

I rise, rubbing at the chilled skin of my arms, and walk.

When I arrive at my house I don't go in the front door. Instead I wander around the side and push open the gate to the backyard, ambling across the grass to a wooden bench situated beneath a huge oak tree.

I slump onto the bench and stare into the warmly lit

windows of my family's kitchen. I can see my mom and dad talking and cooking, can hear the quiet strains of some blues record seeping through the windows. I stare at my family's kitchen full of golden light and warmth and food.

Somewhere nearby a child shouts and giggles. In the distance I can hear the whir and clank of a passing train. A car horn sounds, followed by shouts, then silence. It's September and it feels like winter, chilly and sharp, and leaves crackle under my feet like sparking fire.

I slide my key into the lock of my front door and twist until it clicks. The house smells like dinner, sweet potatoes and chicken and greens. My mom emerges from the kitchen with a tired smile on her face and an apron tied around her waist, dark eyes shimmering. She wraps her arms around me in a hug, and for once, I let her hold me.

"How did things go today?" she asks.

"Good," I say. "I'm alive."

"Well, I should hope so," she says, pulling back and looking into my eyes.

"That Othello dude is pretty messed up," I say, and she laughs.

"He is, baby," she says softly, and brushes a stray curl of my hair out of my eyes. "But you know, he was in love."

Melanie

We fought the day you got the news.

It was a stupid fight too—I don't know what it was about.
*   I don't even remember.*

I was pissed all day, whined at Tristan: My mom is so
*   lame, oh my God, I hate her.*

Tristan just patted me on the arm and said, Let's go buy
*   something, like . . . boots.*

But we didn't go, because Dad called when I was still at
*   school and said I needed to come straight home. You*
*   sat me down at the dining room table and sipped tea*
*   while he said a bunch of words I didn't understand:*
*   Terminal. Progressive. Potentially fatal.*

I did understand two words: CANCER and LATE.

All of a sudden I was angry for different reasons, so
*   angry I wanted to tear down the walls you'd painted*
*   in alternating stripes, purple and blue.*

I wanted to say: How could you not know? Why didn't
*   you go to the doctor more? You always know every-*
*   thing, how could you not know this?*

But there was no space to say that.

There was no time.

You didn't throw things like you used to when you got

angry, lamps and dishes and sometimes even a
painting pulled off the wall. I wanted you to. I
wanted you to break every dish in our kitchen.
I wanted you to scream. I wanted you to be
something other than blank, other than accepting.
I wanted you not to give up.
Why did you give up?

CHAPTER FOUR

Quick. Four guys you'd do at this school." Tristan puts up a hand preemptively. "Four guys who are not me if I was straight."

I open my mouth, then close it, glaring at Tristan.

"That's not fair. I don't like this game."

Tristan flips dark hair out of his eyes and lifts his eyebrows.

"Life isn't fair, Melly. Answer the question."

"I don't like the guys at this school. They're dumb. Can we do movie stars instead?"

Tristan is examining his nails. "You're embarrassing yourself. Just answer the question."

I let my eyes skim the playground. The pickings are slim. There are a bunch of white dudes in one corner near the fence wearing skinny jeans and band T-shirts and kicking around a Hacky Sack. I recognize one of them, Terrence Drake, from my physics class. He's got nice eyes—hazel, with long eyelashes. But he makes people call him "T-Dog" and smells like patchouli, so he's out.

Some guys from the basketball team are playing on the court. A few of them are shirtless, and I can see the way Rihad Jones's muscles tighten when he lifts his arms and releases the ball with a flick of his wrist. The hoop doesn't have a net, but I can hear them making *swish* noises whenever someone makes a shot. Guys who generate their own victorious sound effects? Hoo boy.

But then out of the corner of my eye I see Damon, walking across the blacktop wearing low-slung jeans and a gray polo shirt. He tugs a hand through his hair as if trying to smooth it down.

He turns, his mouth widening into a smile, and lifts one hand in a wave.

"Hey, Melanie," he calls.

I give him this pathetic little half wave in return, a scrunching of my fingers that probably makes me look like I'm physically disabled.

"Well," Tristan says, looking at me with narrowed eyes. "I think we have number one with a bullet."

That afternoon as I get ready to go to work, I stare at the photograph propped up on top of my dresser. Carlos looks out into the middle distance, like he can see something I can't.

Was. He was a cool guy.

Carlos looks like he could be some boy I have class with, some guy I might see hanging around the 7-Eleven, smoking cigarettes and harassing the ladies. Like he could be one of those boys on the basketball court, a choice in one of Tristan's dumb lunchtime games of questions.

But he's not, is he? Because Carlos is not around, period.

Keep it, Damon had said as he slid the photo across the table.

Keep what?

"Mel, you ready?"

"Be down in a minute," I shout down the stairs, and slip on my jacket.

I feel Carlos in the room as I leave, feel him staring at everything but me. I wonder what he sees off in that middle distance: if maybe it's Damon, if maybe he'll let me in on his secrets.

At the restaurant, I settle down in a chair in the kitchen on my break, tugging the grief book out of my backpack and flipping it open.

My aunt Frannie gave me this gem of a book at the funeral, because there is nothing you want to do more after your mom dies than read a book about death.

How are you holding up, sweetheart? Frannie asked, cupping my cheek with one cool palm.

I shrugged. What should I have said? *Not well. Not well at all.*

She was a beautiful woman, Frannie said, sniffling. *She was the best sister and mom anyone could ask for, and that's something. Isn't it?*

Yeah, I murmured. *Yeah, I guess.*

Frannie reached into her purse and pulled out a slim book, which she pressed into my hands. It was coated in plastic, laminated like it was meant to be read in the tub. The cover read *Understanding Grief* in big block letters. I squinted. There were Russian dolls on the cover, the kind that nest inside of each other, maybe some kind of meta-phor about taking apart the layers of sorrow?

Read it, Frannie said.

She pulled me into a hug, the book pressed between us.

After the funeral I left it on my bedside table, deter-mined to never look at it again. But then one night I found myself thinking about my mom and wishing so hard that there was something somewhere that could explain the way I felt, and there it was. *This will be stupid*, I thought, and opened it.

It wasn't.

So I kept reading it, a little bit every night before I went to bed, and then sometimes before school, and then I started carrying it around with me for those moments when I think: *I need some answers.*

Today is one of those days.

I read:

> *Grief is complicated. People who see the griev-ing process as a path toward closure are miss-ing the point. Grief is not about closure; it is about coping in the present. We may spend our entire lives grieving for someone, and this can still be a way of coming to terms with that loss.*

If it's not about closure—if it's not about letting go—then what is it about, exactly? How do we "cope in the present"? Is it about keeping someone close? Because I kept my mom so close those last six months, I sometimes felt like there was no space between us, like we were one and the same. So close I could see all the things the cancer did to her, all the ways it burned her up and tore her apart. So close I would see her on the back of my eyelids every time I closed my eyes and tried to sleep. So close that sometimes I felt like I couldn't breathe because she couldn't breathe. So close I could see life leaving her behind.

I sat by her bedside for all those hours and watched death take her away from me. Now I'm supposed to keep her close?

"You look real busy."

I jump at the low, rumbly voice behind me, but when I turn it's just Macho. He leans against the wall and gives me a crooked smile.

"Not busy. Reading," I say, and close the book with a snap.

"What are you reading?" Macho asks.

I slip the book into my bag on the floor. "Nothing."

Macho gives me a careful look, then slides into the seat next to me.

"I been listening to the new Beyoncé. It's off the hook."

"I'm not against Beyoncé, you know," I say. "But why not Aretha Franklin? Some Etta James?"

"Ain't nothin' wrong with Aretha or Etta," Macho says. "But those ladies don't shake their ass like Beyoncé does. That's all I'm sayin'."

I toss a straw wrapper at him, which he dodges expertly, laughing. "You're an idiot," I say.

"You know something?" he says. He runs one finger over his bottom lip, a thoughtful tick. "You look a lot like your mom when you do that. When you give me the bitchy face, with your eyes all narrow and your eyebrows up."

"Oh, thanks," I say. "Thanks a lot."

But Macho smiles that little smile of his, and I know he means *you got her inside of you, girl.*

The thing about keeping her close—I don't think I get to choose.

Starbucks, four o'clock on a Friday afternoon: Caffein-ated Corporate Wonderland. Two old ladies stare at my scarlet-streaked hair. I consider taking out a couple of my piercings and shoving them up their pointy, lifted noses. It hasn't been a particularly good day. I had gym class. It's never a good day when I have gym class.

"Volleyball was clearly a sport invented by the devil," I tell Tristan. "Satan plays volleyball. Satan loves volleyball. Satan holds volleyball championships in hell, possibly every day."

"Volleyball sucks, it's true," Tristan says. "Are you even listening to me?"

Truth be told, I've been sipping a decaf latte and trying to ignore Tristan, who's drinking nothing at all but bounc-ing like he's inhaled six shots of espresso.

"C'mon, Melanie. Please?"

Tristan is giving me the pretty blue puppy eyes, but that doesn't change the fact that what he's asking me to do is deranged.

"Just let me tell them we're going with your dad to the shore this weekend," Tristan pleads. "They'll believe it, I know they will. They won't like it, but they'll totally believe it, and they won't check either. If I tell them Bryan and I are going to Rehoboth for the weekend and his parents aren't going to be there—"

"Oh, so it's the no-parental-supervision thing? It has nothing to do with the super-queer sex thing?"

Tristan runs his hand through his hair, eyebrows knitting. I sigh.

"Bryan is bi, okay?" Tristan interrupts, looking flustered. "I . . . please. Please."

"Okay, okay, okay," I relent. "Fine. Just . . . make sure they don't call my dad, all right? He's really not in the mood."

Tristan nods emphatically, beaming. "Yes. Of course."

He clears his throat importantly.

"And . . . now let's talk about you, dollface."

I narrow my eyes. "What about me, exactly?"

"Well, firstly, your extreme hardcore crush on Damon Lewis," Tristan says.

"Excuse me?"

Tristan rolls his eyes.

"Look, Mel, I've got eyes, and apparently—thank God, because I was beginning to wonder—you do too. I saw you scoping him out at lunch."

"I was just spacing out."

He nudges me with his shoulder. "You were staring, you

liar. And I know you weren't perving on those other jocks because it's, like, against your religion, so . . ."

"How do you even know Damon?" I ask. "He's new."

"Ha!" Tristan slaps me on the thigh. "You are so busted."

I exhale dramatically. "Fuck you."

"And it might interest you to know," he says, "that I know him because he auditioned for *Othello*."

"Are you serious?"

I don't know why that confuses me so much. Damon, a theater kid? My fake fantasy life was definitely off.

"*So* serious." Tristan grins. "He's very talented, in case you're wondering. He got the lead! And . . ." Tristan pauses, evidently for theatrical effect. "He's not gay."

"You know this how?" I ask.

"I asked him," Tristan says simply.

My mouth falls open. "You're kidding."

"Nope." Tristan shakes his head. "I said, 'Hey, Damon, nice shoes—'"

I put up my hand, fixing him with a dark glare.

"Let us remember that I'm bailing your ungrateful ass out this weekend, you dick."

"I told him, 'Y'know, people might make certain assumptions about you, auditioning for the play—'"

"You didn't. Tristan!" I exclaim.

". . . and he said, 'I'm not gay, and I don't care what people think.'" Tristan's a little breathless. "Seriously, that's what he said, Mel." He lifts an eyebrow. "I can't say I wasn't disappointed, you know. He is beautiful."

I shove him, nearly making him topple out of his chair. "Asshole."

Tristan smiles wickedly.

"You should do something with the play," he hints. "Paint sets, maybe."

"Why would I want to do that?" I ask.

"Because proximity is a good thing," Tristan says. "Plus, you'd be good at it. You've always been good at stuff like that. Like . . . you know." His voice gets softer. "Like your mother."

Like your mother.

When I was in middle school, my mom made me help her paint sets for the munchkin production of *Little Shop of Horrors* that they were putting on at the school where she was teaching art. My mom loved to do that—suggest ludicrous musicals that were totally inappropriate for small children but that would involve awesome sets. Why not eight-year-olds doing *A Chorus Line?* Fifth graders doing *Rent?* There would be at least four PTA meetings a year devoted to dealing with furious parents who thought my mom was a head case. I'm surprised she never got fired.

Those sets were a pain in the butt, but I kind of liked it. Putting paint to a surface, watching the shapes form. Creating the backdrop for the action of theater to take place. I've always been more comfortable being in the background anyway. This gave me an excuse.

My mom even had the decency to pretend she didn't know about the sketchbook I kept under my bed that I'd pull out when I was bored. I'd doodle in it, copying comic book characters out of Tristan's issues of *X-Men* that I knew he read because the dudes in it were so muscly and the costumes were so tight.

Now it seems so stupid, that I kept that from her, that I didn't want her to know how much I loved what she did.

It's been so long since I've looked at that sketchbook, so long since I've drawn anything. I'm weirdly grateful they cut the budget for the arts so we don't have art class this year. I don't think I could sit there in a room of other kids and explain why it makes me want to cry to pick up a pencil and learn figure drawing.

Am I ready for this?

"I'll think about it," I tell him, and he gives me one of his sweetest smiles and squeezes my hand, once, twice.

On Monday, I get cornered by Mrs. McAvoy after third period precalc. She seems to be under the mistaken impression that I will be doing set design for the play.

He might be my best friend, but Tristan is still a little bastard.

"It'd be lovely if you could," Mrs. McAvoy chirps. She's a round, rosy-cheeked woman with an apparently endless supply of enthusiasm and giant earrings. I'm pretty sure she's only been teaching at Hamilton for a couple years, which would explain her currently unconditional love for her job. Give her a few more years and all that passion will be gone, replaced by bitter cynicism and generalized animosity toward all young people. She'll be just another misanthrope slouching her way through the halls, waiting for students to do something stupid so she can yell at them.

"The thing is, I'm really busy right now—" I lie.

"It would only be a few afternoons a week. You could even do it on weekends. And I'd make sure you got extra credit in English."

She blinks up at me expectantly, still smiling.

"I don't know, it's . . ."

I hear my mom say: *You never let them in, Melly.*

"Come by after four today and I'll show you what it would involve, and you can decide then," she says. "It's so much fun! You'll love it."

She bustles off down the hall, leaving me standing there, slack-jawed and confused.

Goddammit. What the hell just happened?

"I hate you," I inform Tristan at lunch.

He blinks at me.

"Ah," he says. "So you talked with Mrs. McAvoy then."

"Yeah, I did," I say. "She's pushy as hell. As are you, by the way. I said I'd think about it!"

"You did say that," Tristan says, "but sometimes you need to be . . . gently encouraged to do something."

"More like coerced," I say.

"Toe-may-toe, toe-mah-toe," Tristan says, and wiggles his eyebrows.

I sigh, but before I can get more irate he begins to fill me in about his weekend away with Bryan.

"Seriously, though, Rehoboth Beach, when nobody's around and you don't have to deal with all the whiny children eating snow cones? Is beautiful."

"Like you were even registering your surroundings," I tease. "You know you and Bryan never left the house."

"We did so leave the house!" Tristan insists. "We had dinner out. Twice."

I snort and push peas around on my plate. They're squishy and gross and I can't bring myself to eat them, even if they are the only part of my lunch that might actually contain nutrients.

"So did you have sex?" I ask.

"Define 'sex.'" Tristan sounds pissy, and has flushed to the color of a carnation.

"Were parts of your body inserted into parts of his body? Or vice versa?"

"If I stuck my finger in his ear that would be true," Tristan retorts. "Is that . . . finger sex?"

"Finger sex, I believe, is different," I say, winking.

"Oh, you're so gross," Tristan says.

"And you are so avoiding the question. I say—no, you did not have sex. This is my assessment."

"We sort of had sex."

"How did you 'sort of' have sex?" I ask. "I want to know what 'sort of' happened, especially since I was your alibi for the weekend."

"We didn't have, like, the all-the-way kind of sex. We had—there were hands involved."

Tristan is so red now. It's kind of hilarious.

"Oh my God, you're a nun!" I says. "I'm surprised you did anything other than soulfully stare into each other's eyes all weekend, you weirdo."

Tristan stares morosely at his half-eaten meat loaf. "I hate you a lot."

He reaches out to take one of my fries, but I swat his hand away. "No way, buddy! Not now that I know where your hands have been!"

That afternoon I make my way to play rehearsal, feeling a little anxious. The auditorium smells like dust and old sweat. The only lights come from the stage; they're big bright ones suspended from the ceiling, perched at angles. By the time I get there at 4:15 p.m. a bunch of kids are already milling around with scripts in their hands, giggling and roughhousing and being silly.

I spot Damon standing on a corner of the stage with Tristan. They're talking intently, heads bowed together, and Tristan places one hand on Damon's arm. Damon laughs, and it's lovely: the way his shoulders move, the slow curve of his smile. Tristan says something and Damon turns to look right at me, lifting his hand to wave. I wave back.

"Oh, splendid, you came!" Mrs. McAvoy is suddenly at my elbow, smiling so widely, I can practically see her molars.

"Melanie, I'll take you backstage and let Calvin show you the ropes."

So much for giving me a chance to decide. Also, Calvin? Nobody mentioned there would be a Calvin. I'm suspicious of anyone named Calvin who does not have a stuffed tiger named Hobbes. It's probably because I knew this kid in third grade named Calvin who ate his own boogers. Entirely traumatic and gross, that kid.

Mrs. McAvoy leads me down the aisle and around the side of the stage, pulling back the curtains so I can see backstage. It looks like a place that old wood goes to retire, like Boca Raton for cedar and pine. I guess this is all going to resemble sets at some point, but right now it looks like the remnants of a salvage mission on some strange all-forest planet.

"Calvin will make you right at home," Mrs. McAvoy says, and just like that, *poof*, she's gone.

"Who are you?" a voice comes out of the darkness. I jump.

"I'm Melanie," I say. "Are you Calvin?"

A boy steps out of the shadows. He's tall and thin, with a narrow face and long, stringy hair dyed jet black. He's wearing a long-sleeve black shirt under a green T-shirt that reads *Fly, my pretties, fly* and ripped blue jeans.

"That is my earth name, yes," Calvin says.

Oh, Jesus.

"Mrs. McAvoy wants me to help with the sets," I say.

Calvin stares at me. His eyes are dark gray and flat, like he's never seen anything that impressed him, ever.

"Have you painted sets before?" he asks.

"Yes," I say. "It was for this elementary school—"

"But not for a Hamilton High production," he says, in the same tone of voice that someone might say *Tony Award–winning Broadway play.*

"Um," I say. "No."

"So why did you decide to start now?"

I guess the answer *because my best friend is a conniving little bastard and there's a boy in the play who's really hot* would not endear me any further to Calvin.

I shrug. "Could use the extra credit."

Calvin appears to be considering this.

"There are easier ways to get extra credit," he says.

Calvin seems to think we are embarking on a top-secret operation into the jungles of Cambodia with the Green Berets, not putting some shellac on a bunch of old lumber vaguely shaped to look like a castle.

"Well, tell me what I'd have to do," I say, "and then I'll decide if I'm up for it."

Calvin narrows his eyes as if to say *you will never be up for what I have to teach you,* but he hands me a brush.

We're doing basic undercoat stuff, but it's amazing how much it shakes me to be holding a paintbrush again. In my mind I keep seeing the canvases in the basement, the piles of them, wondering: *Where will they all go now?* I wouldn't even know how to ask my dad about that. Where would my mom want them to go? I think about the way she looked toward the end when I would bring her paper and pencil. She would stare at it for minutes that felt like they lasted hours, then say: *I can't, Melly. Not today.*

About an hour has passed when Calvin sidles up behind me, cocks his head to one side and says, "You may take a break."

I swallow a nasty retort and wander out into the theater.

Rehearsal is in full swing, and Damon is up onstage along with a couple other guys. He stands tall and regal.

> *She swore, in faith, 'twas strange, 'twas passing strange,*
> *'Twas pitiful, 'twas wondrous pitiful.*
> *She wished she had not heard it, yet she wished*
> *That heaven had made her such a man.*

Oh, vomit. I remember this now: the gorgeous fragile flower Desdemona, wilting in Othello's arms. I always hated Desdemona, how ditzy and useless she seemed to be.

But then Damon's voice drops, and he looks up and out at the audience, and—

> *I should but teach him how to tell my story,*
> *And that would woo her. Upon this hint I spake.*
> *She loved me for the dangers I had passed,*
> *And I loved her that she did pity them.*
> *This only is the witchcraft I have used.*
> *Here comes the lady. Let her witness it.*

Before he turns toward the wings where Desdemona is emerging, I could swear that Damon catches my eye. The moment lasts only a split second, but in that second I think: *I want, I want, I want you to tell me your story.*

I want to know the story behind the photograph of this boy with laughing eyes that sits propped up on my dresser beside my jewelry box. I want to know the story of the boy who took the photograph. Who bore witness.

I want to know what he saw, know what he knows.

But do I want him to know my story? The story of Melanie Ellis, who for years used to wear boring clothes and her hair flat and brown so she could disappear? Who used to draw in secret because she knew she'd never be as good as her rock star of a mother, her mother who is—

I stop. I make myself stop.

I am not going to cry here.

I have to stop.

I put down my shades. I close all my doors.

After rehearsal I'm gathering up my stuff when I see Damon approach, bag already slung over his shoulder. He lifts his camera and snaps a picture of the empty stage, then tucks it into his bag.

He looks up at me.

"Hey," he says.

"Hey," I reply.

"I didn't mean to freak you out," he says. "At the restaurant. I didn't mean—"

"You didn't freak me out," I say. "You ditched me. I could take it personally, but I'm choosing to think it's just because you're weird."

Damon flushes, and dammit if he isn't especially cute when he's embarrassed.

"It wasn't personal," he says. "I'm just weird."

"Now that I know that you're a theater geek, your weirdness makes so much more sense."

He gives me a wry look.

"I guess you can't be that freaked out. You're here too, after all."

"I'm here under extreme duress," I say. "Tristan's a punk and he's forcing me to paint sets."

"Tristan wears a lot of Abercrombie for a punk," Damon says, lifting an eyebrow.

"He's an asshole," I say stubbornly.

Damon's mouth quirks.

"I think he's all right," Damon says. "And I'm guessing that if he's forcing you to paint sets, it's because he thinks you'd be good at it."

"I guess," I say.

I can't go there now. Not with him. Not like this.

We stand awkwardly for a moment, and Damon runs a hand through his hair.

"I do think we should hang out," Damon says. "I mean, outside of the restaurant. Outside of school. With me seeming less like a stalker."

"Can you promise me you won't run away this time?" I ask.

Damon's digging into his pocket for his phone. He hands it to me and I type in my number, then hand it back to him. He swipes open the camera app and snaps my picture.

That camera's on me for sure now.

"I promise," he says.

At the restaurant that afternoon I drift off in the middle of putting in an order while thinking about Damon, so intense up there on that stage, his body shaping itself around words hundreds of years old. He'd been so right in that moment, so perfect in that scene. So real.

"Mel." An elbow digs into my side. I blink and turn to see Macho standing there, a smirk turning up the corners of his mouth.

"You been—" he says, pinching his fingers together and lifting them to his mouth.

I shove him, hard.

"No, you ass," I say, but to be honest I do feel drugged, brain fogged over and mushy.

I remember going to a party at Alyssa Franco's house with Tristan last year (I only ever go to parties when Tristan "gently encourages" me) and a dude named Graham offered me a joint before we even got in the door.

You smoke, Ellis? he said.

I was surprised he knew my last name.

No thank you, I said.

No thank you, Graham mimicked, except he made his voice all high and prim, like I was some kind of uptight librarian.

I don't want any, okay? I said.

It's too bad, he said. *'Cause you need to relax, lady.*

I just stared at him and then turned and walked away. I went to find Tristan, and then I made him take me home.

The first time I actually got high was with my mom this summer. We smoked together after she got some doctor to prescribe her weed for the nausea.

You want some? she asked me after she lit up, and I looked at her like she was crazy.

Really? I said.

Really, she said. *It won't hurt you, Melly.*

So I did it. It didn't seem so strange in those moments, somehow, because everything was strange. I was getting high with my mom, yes, but my mom was also dying. It's hard to be concerned about societal conventions when your mother is fading from this world like a bruise.

The weed didn't hurt me. She was right about that. It made me cough and I felt kind of dizzy, but then it was nice. It was so nice not worrying about anything for a while. I would sit next to my mom and watch her sleep, and sometimes I'd take out my sketch pad and draw her. It was easier to draw like that, when I wasn't worrying about what somebody would think, whether it was good enough.

The weird thing about art, Melly, my mom told me once, *is that you make it for the world, but when you're making it, you have to stop thinking about that. You have to stop caring about what people might say about it, or who might buy it. Because if you think about it too much, you can't create. You're paralyzed.*

So how do you stop caring, then? I said.

My mom shrugged.

I don't know, she said. *You just do.*

"Well, wake up then, girl," Macho says, and pats me affectionately on the cheek, pulling me back into the present. "Order up on table three."

That night I lie in bed, feeling restless and annoyed. I shift against my pillow, staring up at the ceiling.

"This sucks," I address the ceiling. "And I know what you'd say. You'd say, 'Oh, you're being silly, Damon's just a boy. He may be cute, but he's just as confused as you are, and you're probably smarter than he is anyway.' But." I sigh. "I like him a lot, and I don't even know him, which is so dumb! He could be a serial killer. He could! Shut up, I know you're laughing, Mom."

I rub at my eyes. It's 3:00 a.m. I need to sleep, but I want my mom to know about this, and I'm pretty sure she's only around late at night. More times than I can count I'd wake up to the sound of a clatter downstairs, get freaked out and inch down the stairs with a baseball bat in hand only to find Mom standing in front of a canvas, examining it thoughtfully, paint in her hair. My mother would look at me like I was the crazy one, her head cocked to one side.

Looking for something? she'd ask, and I would huff out, *Yeah, I thought we were being robbed.*

I look down at my tank top. It's nearly see-through, and the dark pink of my areolas is visible through the ribbed fabric. When I first got boobs in fifth grade, I thought they were sort of awesome. Now I kind of hate them. I'm not sure if it's because I've changed or because the boys haven't.

Mom was so unafraid of her own body and of anybody else's. I know there are canvases in her studio of her, naked, painted when she was in art school. *Everybody did it, honey*, she told me as I stared in horror, partly because it was my mom! Naked! But also because I couldn't imagine it, couldn't imagine being like her—so bold, not caring what anyone else thinks.

Once, we were out shopping for jeans, an exercise in humiliation and self-abuse if there ever was one, and we'd suspended the disastrous quest in favor of smoothies at Jamba Juice: Strawberry Whirl for my mom, Mega Mango for me. I'd asked my mom to tell me the story of how she'd met my dad in college. I'd heard it before, but I wanted to hear her tell it again. My mom stirred the thick liquid of her drink, lips curving into a small smile.

It was an art class, she'd said. *Can you believe your dad took an art class?*

That part always cracked me up. It was funny to think about my dad as a junior Rembrandt.

He came up to me and said what I was painting was good, Mom had continued. *I told him I liked it a lot myself, that I wanted to be a painter. He said he needed the art credit.*

"Oh, really?" I said. "Well, that's honest."

He said, "I'm an honest kind of guy." He looked really cute when he said it too, very earnest. You know, like he meant it. And he did. That's your daddy in a nutshell, Melanie. He means it. When it matters, he does. But you know what, Mel? It wasn't like I knew, then—like I knew in some crazy cosmic way that we belonged together or anything like that. Just—when I met him, I knew something was different. That my world had changed.

I think of that moment in the woods, with Damon. Had my world changed in that moment, without me even realizing it?

I wish so much that I could ask my mom about this. How do I even explain this to anyone, the frustration I feel when I want to ask her questions and she's not here?

The rest of my life I'm going to wonder what she would have thought, and I will never know.

Sunday morning my cell phone rings while I'm chatting online with Tristan, having a serious and complex discussion about what pair of boots Tristan should ask for for his birthday. This is why I don't look at my phone before I answer.

"Hey, Melanie, what's up?"

My stomach does a skipping flip. "Oh—hi, Damon. How are—how are you?"

Great. I sound like I've just learned English.

"Pretty good, though things could be better," he says. "You know how they could be better?"

hey, i asked you a question, my chat window beeps. where'd you go?

I minimize the window. Tristan will understand. *You are always allowed to ditch me for a hot boy,* Tristan told me once. *Unless you're stealing my boyfriend. Then we'll have to have words.*

"How could your Sunday be better?" I ask, recovering in an admirable fashion. "Do tell."

"You could hang out with me later."

"Later?"

"Around, oh, twenty minutes from now."

"Twenty minutes? Are you serious?"

Oh, the presumption. But like I'm going to say no.

"Serious as a heart attack."

"You want to go to a movie or something?" I ask. That would be okay. Low pressure. Not many opportunities for conversation.

"Meet me at the zoo, the north entrance on Connecticut."

"But I—"

"Oh, and bring good shoes."

"What are you—"

My phone's already gone dead. I stare at it for a moment before slipping it into my pocket, then yanking on my sneakers.

Let them in, Melly—

But as I walk to the zoo, I find myself considering the possibilities that might await me there. Damon could be crazy! The National Zoo on a Sunday doesn't strike me as a particularly auspicious place to carve someone up, though. Too many tourists and babies in strollers.

Maybe he has a weird giraffe fetish.

Maybe he's like every other teenage boy on the face

of the earth and thinks it's hilarious to freak people out with the giant boa constrictor in the reptile house that only eats whole live mice and takes days to digest them, lying coiled up and enormous in its cage with a lump in the middle of its body.

I shudder. Now I'm officially freaked out, and I haven't even gotten to the zoo yet. Awesome.

I want to seem cool and smart and witty with Damon, to act like hot boys invite me to the zoo all the time: *Oh yeah, whatever, this is what I always do on Sunday afternoons.* But I'm not the actor, Damon is. Mostly I'm petrified, because Damon is hot, and I'm clumsy and awkward and not nearly hot enough. I'm not my mom. I'm still that girl, the one trying to blend into corners. *Don't be fooled, Damon!* I want to tell him. *Just because my hair is streaked red doesn't mean I'm hot.*

All of these things make me want to turn on my heel and run, run all the way back home and climb into my bed under the covers and lie there for the rest of the day feeling like a loser.

But I refuse to be that lame, dammit. I may be a spaz, but I am not that much of a pussy.

Damon's standing near the entranceway beneath the iron arch that proclaims *National Zoo* in large baroque letters. He's got his hands stuffed into the pockets of a navy blue windbreaker and he's looking at the ground, his dark hair messy. I tuck a thumb into my belt loop, tugging up my jeans—not even the cutest ones I own. I wish I was wearing something nicer, something tighter or more low-cut, but he only gave me twenty minutes and—

Then Damon looks up and sees me and his mouth tips into a lazy grin, and suddenly I don't wish that at all.

"What's goin' on, girl?" he says as I approach.

"Not much, not much," I say.

He watches me with his pretty eyes. He doesn't look away when I look at him; he just stares, holding my gaze. Most people don't like making eye contact, but Damon doesn't seem to mind. *People who look into your eyes are more likely to tell the truth,* Tristan told me once. He'd been watching FBI documentaries, so Lord knows, but maybe. Maybe it's true.

"So where are we going?" I ask. "I've been to the zoo before, you know. The pandas don't hold quite the same mystique as they did when I was four years old."

"Oh," Damon says, "we're not going to the zoo."

What the fuck.

"C'mon," Damon says, and tugs on my sleeve.

I don't know why I follow without protest or objection, but I do. It's like I'm in a daze. I follow him as he leads me past the tapirs, past the monkey house and the gift shop with the world's largest supply of stuffed animals and books on the mating habits of lizards and the different patterns of leopard spots, past the food stands serving funnel cake and lemonade, past about a hundred thousand screaming, crying, shouting children. We stumble down a hill off the main path, and all of a sudden we're in the woods behind the zoo, D.C.'s little section of preserved wilderness: Rock Creek Park.

My mom loved this park. She loved how green it was, how the light cut through the trees and made patterns on the forest floor.

Feeling the carpet of green mush under my feet and watching the tree branches sway in the wind reminds me of those times when I felt like I was one with my surroundings, like my arms were streaked with the veins of leaves, like I could photosynthesize light into energy by standing beneath the sun. Before the hospital became my second home, I would come here all the time when I needed to think, to process. I'd crouch on a mossy spot and draw, often trees because they were there right above me. The endlessly varied shapes of trees, no two the same. Every single one with a different story.

I didn't worry about anything else then. Not when I was drawing.

So how do you stop caring, then?

I don't know. You just do.

"I thought we could try this again," Damon says. "With less tears and weirdness."

I realize: This is where we met.

I turn in a circle, watching the light filter through the branches in the canopy above, coming down in sparkling sheets.

"It's so alive, you know?" Damon says. "Everything around here is alive."

"It's beautiful," I whisper.

"I used to come here with Carlos a lot," Damon says. "It felt like an escape, being here. Like we were—I don't know. Explorers. That probably sounds mad stupid."

"No," I say. "It is like a whole other world. It feels like you're not even in the city anymore."

"Yeah," Damon says. He looks distant.

"It's a good place to take pictures too," I say, hoping to bring him back. "You always have that camera."

He's got the camera with him right now, slung over his shoulder.

Damon looks startled, but then he recovers.

"It is," he says. "I think—I take pictures 'cause it makes you look close."

Look close. Maybe that's what Damon's trying to do when he watches me so carefully, trying to frame me, break me down to my parts. I like watching people too, sometimes, in the restaurant or on the bus or in Dupont or at school, taking them apart and putting them back together piece by piece. Observing the way a man twists his wrist or stretches his arm, the way a child's legs scissor when they run, the way a woman bites her nails or adjusts her shoe strap or flips her hair.

My mother used to tell me that. *Look close.*

Damon sits down on a rock and gestures for me to do the same. When I'm situated, he says, "So your dad owns the restaurant, but where's your mom?"

Gone to a better place?

No. Just gone.

"She's dead," I say. "She died this summer. Cancer."

Damon sucks in a breath. "Oh."

"Yeah. It's kind of a conversation stopper."

"So when I saw you before—when you were crying—"

I nod and scratch the toe of my shoe in the dirt, saying nothing.

"I never know what to say except that I'm—I'm sorry. That must be rough. I can't even really imagine how rough that is."

The silence hangs over us for a full minute, and in the background I can hear the swish of the wind through the trees and the muted rumble of traffic from the parkway, a reminder of the city that's never far away. I think I understand what's meant by a "pregnant pause" now. The moment feels like it's swollen with something that's waiting to come out, that from this moment, something should be born.

"You okay?" Damon asks, and his hand falls on my back, landing between my shoulder blades.

He's touching me. He asked me a question. Shit. What question did he ask?

"I don't know," I say.

That may be the first time I've answered that question honestly since my mom died.

"You seem pretty together," he says. "I mean, considering you lost your mother only this summer."

"Yeah, well," I start to say, then realize I don't know what I want to say.

What was I supposed to do? Fall apart? That never seemed

like an option, somehow. People do fall apart. I know that. The grief book certainly knows that. But I never saw it that way, never thought: *I can be a mess. I'm allowed to be a mess.* I know Mom wouldn't have wanted that. If there was one thing my mother taught me and taught me well, it was how to hold myself together even when I feel broken and messy and awful, like a carton of eggs turned over on the kitchen floor, leaking sticky yolk into the grout between the tile.

"I don't know if I can be okay right now," I say. "You know?"

Damon looks at me, his eyes the green of fresh-cut grass.

"Yeah," he says. "I know."

"Carlos," I say. "You said he was—you said 'was.'"

Damon looks up. His eyes have that faraway look they had at the restaurant when he slid the photograph across the table, the same look he had the first time we met.

The look he has as Othello, up on that stage.

"Yeah," Damon says. "He was my best friend, but he's gone now."

There is a story there, I know it, and it's a story I want him to tell. I want to ask him: *How? How is he gone?*

She loved me for the dangers I had passed.

I have so many questions, but I bite them back. Damon is staring at the ground like he wants to be under it.

Maybe words are overrated, and this is what we're supposed to be doing right now, this and nothing else. I reach across the space between us and take Damon's hand, feel his palm smooth against my own, and hold on.

DAMON

*That show at the 9:30 Club, the first show we ever went
    to together . . . what was it, man? I don't even
    remember what we went to see. I know it was all
    ages and we were thirteen and my mom dropped
    us off outside and she was freaked out, like, Don't
    do anything stupid, don't get mugged, don't talk
    to anybody, don't, don't, don't. And yeah, that
    neighborhood is not the best, but we laughed so
    hard after,* you gasping out, Shit, dude, what if
    I want some water at the bar, can I ask the
    bartender or do I have to pull my glock?
I do remember. *It was a hip-hop show, all bass and
    beats, and we got so close to the stage, our whole
    bodies vibrated with it. You kept your hand on
    my shoulder and mouthed all the words and after-
    ward our T-shirts were sweated through from all
    the close bodies, the jumping up and down and
    dancing and screaming.*
We have to do that again, *you said, your voice hoarse,
    and we waited outside for my mom to pick us up,
    leaning against the wall. We watched people stream
    by all high off music, the sky above us dark and
    shimmering, raised voices disappearing into the night.*

CHAPTER FIVE

walk Melanie home. We don't talk much. Mostly we look—not at each other, but around us at trees weeping leaves, shoppers getting in and out of cars with straining plastic grocery bags, people walking dogs on taut leashes, yelling at their kids. Sometimes we catch each other looking at the same things, and our eyes meet, and we smile.

"My house is this way," she tells me, and leads me down a leafy, shaded block of modest homes. Her house is a bungalow, smaller than my family's house, painted blue and white with a neatly groomed front lawn. It looks comfortable, plenty large enough for two people. Even, I suppose, for three.

"I like that place," Melanie says.

I want to like it. I want to like it the way I used to like it, before—

"Thank you for today," Melanie says, and takes my hand again. Her palm is cool against mine, her skin soft.

"Thank *you*," I say.

Melanie tips her head to one side, looks at me with bright eyes, and smiles.

At play rehearsal the next day, I prepare in my usual way: Etta on my iPod, camera in my hands. I snap some photos of the partially constructed set, admiring the way it's already coming together, pieces and fragments joining to create a complete picture.

Othello, however, remains in shards in my mind. I should have known that doing this play would make me angry. *Othello* is a play filled with anger, after all, a play about a man undone by his own anger and his inability to control or direct it. I've never thought of myself as an angry person, but now with each day that Mrs. McAvoy blocks out the play, I get more furious at the people who deceive Othello. The anger seeps into my performance and Mrs. McAvoy loves it, eats it up and eggs me on, tells me to "keep digging, keep pushing, honey!"

The cast seems to love it too. There's nothing more surreal than Lacey Andrews hanging off my arm bubbling over with enthusiasm, telling me, "God, Damon, you're so hot up there."

People think you're all sexy when you're angry, Carlos told me once when we were washing his car, a beat-up truck he'd bought off his uncle for $500. *What the hell is that about? Like anger is passion. Like anger is . . . sex.*

Like anger is primitive, I replied. *That's why there's all that crazy shit about how slaves were more sexually potent or whatever. More like animals.*

Makes sense, kinda, Carlos said, flipping a dirty towel over his shoulder. *I mean, the sex and anger part. Both things make us more conscious of how we're like animals. Our base instincts and shit.*

I wonder, now, what Carlos knew about his own instincts, about his own anger.

God. I wonder so many things.

When my thoughts twist into a mess at rehearsal, I find Melanie. On break we sit together backstage and chat about anything and nothing and everything in between.

"Peanut butter," Melanie says.

"What?"

"If I had to live on one substance forever. Peanut butter."

"Not chocolate? Wouldn't you get all sticky from peanut butter?"

"What would you eat then, genius?"

"Macaroni and cheese."

Melanie laughs. "That is not a single food."

"It is the way my mom makes it."

"I don't know if I should be impressed or scared."

"You should come by sometime," I say. "Try it out."

Oh, man. I think I just invited her over to my house.

"Well, you made it sound so appetizing . . ." Melanie jokes, and I bump her shoulder with mine.

"What's going down back here, kids?" Tristan pokes his head around the curtain.

"Damon's invading my personal space," Melanie says.

"She likes it," I say.

"Lies," Melanie mutters.

"This makes me want to go to Venice," Tristan says, tilting his head to one side to examine the scenery.

"You just like Italian boys," Melanie retorts.

"That too," Tristan says, smirking. "Italy is very aesthetically pleasing."

"Venice stretches across a hundred eighteen small islands in the Venetian Lagoon," I inform them. "That's along the Adriatic Sea."

Melanie looks at me with raised eyebrows. "You're kind of a geek, aren't you? Secretly, inside?"

"Take away the secretly and inside part, then yes," I say, and Melanie laughs.

"There's this exhibit at the National Gallery on Venetian art from the 1500s," Tristan says thoughtfully. "My art teacher was talking about it. We should check it out."

I imagine Othello, walking around the palace in Venice, gazing at the art on the walls, the paintings as foreign to him as he was to the Venetians.

"That could be cool," I say.

"Let's go to the museum on Sunday," Melanie says. "It'll be like school, but on a weekend."

"Totally wild and crazy," Tristan adds.

"Sounds excellent," I say, and I mean it.

The National Gallery towers over us, a giant neoclassical monolith of a building. The place has always looked like a temple to me, a venue to worship art in its many forms. We wander inside, and I take some photos of the cream-colored walls and hardwood and marble. Enormous black columns rise up before us, white lines slithering over their smooth surfaces. We climb the winding marble staircases to find the open space in the center, always filled with plants, a huge ivory-encased greenhouse.

We're scheduled to meet up with the infamous Bryan here. Melanie and Tristan wander off to marvel at an enormous spider plant, while I thumb through the postcards in the exhibit gift shop.

"Damon," Bryan says, and we bump fists.

Bryan looks different without Tristan's hand down his pants: less ruffled, more smug.

"Bryan," I say. "Nice to actually meet you."

Bryan flushes. "Same to you."

"You a fan of Venetian art?" I ask.

Bryan's staring over my shoulder, and I follow his gaze to see Tristan, who's standing with Melanie by the table of gift books and laughing. Tristan's smile is contagious. He smiles with his whole face, eyes bright and cheeks stretched wide.

"Yeah," Bryan says. "Something like that."

Tristan turns, sees us, and bounds over. "Let's go in. There's Tit-tian to be seen."

"Did you just say something dirty?" Bryan asks, and Tristan wraps his hand around Bryan's wrist and tugs him along.

"I hope you didn't come expecting excitement," Melanie says. "It is a museum, you know."

"Museums can be exciting," I say.

I incline my head toward Bryan and Tristan, who are holding hands. Tristan whispers something into Bryan's ear, and Bryan goes so pink, he's almost purple.

Melanie makes a face. "Gross. Let's go learn something about art."

The exhibit is fascinating. It's all about color, the differences between how painters in Venice were tinting and adding tone and dimension to their work. After a while, the images blur together into a sea of warm shades and faded landscapes.

Then one catches my eye, digs its fingers in and holds me still.

It's a reproduction of a fresco that is painted on the walls of Scuola del Santo in Padua, part of a series on the life of Saint Anthony. The title is *The Miracle of the Jealous Husband*. The composition is strange: The entire top half of the painting is a landscape, displaying a mountain with spindly trees poking out of it. The colors are cool and quiet, grays and blues, peaceful. In the right-hand corner there are three small figures, nearly indistinct, but pictured in the bottom half are two very distinct figures: a man wearing a red-and-white-striped tunic belted at the waist, and a woman, sprawled on the ground below him, in a dress of vibrant orange-yellow. The man holds a knife in one hand, and she has one arm flung out to keep him at a distance.

I get it, suddenly. She's trying to keep him from killing her. It is a painting of brutal, anticipatory slaughter. He's stabbed her but now they are both frozen, destined to spend forever preparing for a final blow that will never come.

"Wow," Melanie says, and I jump. I turn to look at her, and there is sadness in her eyes.

"Yeah," I say. "Exactly."

"You forget, sometimes," Melanie says, "that he does that. Othello. I mean, you don't forget, but you don't think about the reality of it, the fact that he kills his wife. In a lot of productions Desdemona just sort of wilts under him, goes to sleep, and then she's so beautiful laid out on that bed, and—"

Melanie stops. Her lips twist as if she's swallowed something bitter.

"I don't ever forget," I say softly, then realize how harsh that sounds. "I mean—"

She places a hand on my arm and squeezes, just once: *I know.*

We take in the rest of the exhibit in silence, the low murmur of voices of the surrounding tourists providing constant white noise. All of the images are interesting, but none make me feel the way *The Miracle of the Jealous Husband* did—desperate and afraid, like I was that woman on the ground fending off the descending knife.

"Kind of amazing, isn't it?" Melanie says. "That's one thing I like about paintings: You can show people what's on your mind, what no one else can see. It's harder to do that with a camera, I think. You have to create something new out of what's already there."

I think of what's still in that box of photos in my closet. I think of the photos I've pasted all over my bedroom walls. Those photos are what Carlos left behind, and yet what really matters are the things I can never see or know, the tangled fantasies that existed only inside Carlos's head.

I have lost Carlos's mind.

"But you can still make people see things in different ways," I say. "Make them see what they didn't on first glance."

"Yeah," Melanie says. Her eyes are heavy. "Let's go outside. Please?"

We leave Tristan and Bryan to flirt their way through the exhibit and wander down the circular staircase, out and around to the Sculpture Garden. Many of the sculptures are strange and modern, in diametric opposition to the exhibit we've just seen. A Louise Bourgeois spider sculpture sends tingles down my spine—the long, thin legs support the hovering arachnid, and it towers over our heads as if ready to lunge out and grab us.

Why does everything seem so menacing today?

Everything but Melanie.

"I like how in the winter they turn this into an ice skating rink," Melanie says as we settle onto a bench. "It makes everything all smooth and pretty."

"Yeah," I murmur.

I know I'm not being much of a conversationalist, but my throat is dry and nothing's making sense right now.

"My mom loved it here in the spring. I'd come down with her a lot," Melanie says. "She liked to draw out here, when the cherry blossoms and magnolias were out. She'd lug this big old sketch pad so she could try to capture the shape of the petals and the exact color of pink around the edges."

"So your mom was an artist?" I ask.

"Yeah," Melanie says. She flushes a little, and I think of those magnolias and cherry blossoms with their pink edges.

"Like you," I say.

Melanie looks up, startled.

"No, not—I mean, I'm not an artist. Not like her."

"But you're doing the sets—"

"I'm not like her," Melanie says, her voice sharp, and I stop.

It's quiet for a moment. I know she's not telling me everything, but how can I ask her to tell me these things when I'm keeping so many secrets of my own?

"In fifth grade we took a field trip here to see the Degas, and Carlos climbed into the fountain with his new water-proof camera," I say.

I remember watching Carlos standing under the spray, grinning, so thrilled with himself even as the security guard ducked under the cascade of water to drag him out.

"Carlos was like that," I continue. "There were so many times they called security or the cops on us because he was trying to take some picture, like, dangling from the bottom of Chain Bridge or some shit."

"Carlos took photos?"

That description just slipped out—that memory, so easy to share with someone else who was remembering too.

"Yeah," I say. "Carlos was more of a photographer than I am, actually."

"Oh," Melanie says.

We sit like that for a few minutes, each watching the air for our separate ghosts. I try to breathe normally. I can feel Melanie beside me breathing too, her inhales and exhales slow and steady.

I know she wants to ask. Everyone does, even when they don't say it. They want to know how. He was seventeen. It's the natural thing to wonder. *How did he die?*

But I don't want to tell her.

"Carlos was a total shit-starter," I say. "Stubborn as hell and . . . kind of an asshole, you know? But in a good way."

Melanie laughs a little. "Those are the best kind."

"I think it made him a good photographer, though," I say. "Because he was fearless."

Melanie's watching me. Up close her eyes have gold in them. For some reason that makes me want to kiss her.

"My mom always seemed pretty fearless," Melanie says. "Like maybe that's what you need to be to create art."

"Theater's like that," I say. "I mean . . . to be a good actor I think maybe you need to be fearless."

"Or just *act* fearless," Melanie says. "It's like that quote: 'Courage is not the absence of fear, but the mastery of it.'"

"Like you never stop being afraid, you just don't let it stop you."

"Yeah," Melanie says. "Exactly."

The wind whips up around us, making me shiver.

For someone so fearless, Carlos sure was afraid of something.

"Are you okay?" Melanie asks.

"Yeah, I'm fine," I say.

So automatic, the way people say that.

"Hey," Melanie says, and takes my hand in hers and squeezes.

I look down at our fingers, intertwined.

Hey. Hey.

As I walk home from Melanie's house that afternoon, an image hits me hard and fast, no warning: Carlos, knees pulled up to his chest, strands of his sweaty hair stuck to his forehead. Post-crew practice, an early morning on a day like today, warm for fall but with an occasional cooler breeze, a preview of the months to come. Everything a vivid green. Sun cut through the trees and Carlos plucked grass out of the ground, single blades and then tufts and handfuls.

Hey, man, don't do that, I said. *You're gonna mess it up.*

Carlos snorted, but he stopped, hands wandering to his thighs and tapping out an uneven beat.

We gotta go to school, I said. *Class in twenty minutes, and I gotta grab a shower.*

You go, Carlos said.

You can't miss more class, I said. *Mrs. Taylor is gonna fail your ass.*

Carlos shrugged. *Let her fail me then.*

You realize that you aren't hurting anybody but yourself, I said.

Carlos stared straight ahead, his brown eyes flat.

Yeah, Carlos said. *I realize.*

So why do you—

You could stay, Carlos said. His hand fell to my arm and squeezed. *We could just stay here.*

Dude, I can't, I said.

Carlos curled his lip and looked away.

What do you want from me? I wanted to say. *What do you want—*

I stab my key into the lock on our front door with unintentional violence. I can hear my mom inside, talking to my dad. The TV's on in the living room—football, probably, Dad watching the Redskins game.

If Carlos were here, we'd probably drive out to Montgomery Mall, wander around and mess with stuff we couldn't afford, harass the piano player at Nordstrom until he played "Für Elise." Carlos loved that song. So weird.

We'd catch a movie, throw popcorn at the screen, maybe get kicked out. Carlos would hit on some salesclerk at Macy's or the french fry girl in the food court and miraculously walk away with her number. Carlos was like that: charming.

But somehow Carlos still managed to be an outsider, an observer. Always the one holding the camera. Never the one connecting. He never seemed to call those girls when he got their numbers, or if he did they only lasted one date, maybe two. He never let anyone close.

Nobody but me.

But did he ever let me that close?

I keep thinking that if I dig down far enough I'll understand why. Why didn't he tell me what was going on, how desperate he was, how afraid? Why did he never let me in?

Was I just dumb, or willfully blind? Why didn't I see what was happening to him? Between us? It's like digging in the rain: The more I dig, the muddier it gets. I'm so tired of being the punch line of a joke I don't get. I feel like giving up, washing my hands until the water runs clean.

On Monday Melanie finds me before rehearsal backstage, sitting with my back against the wall, earphones wedged in my ears, listening to Ray Charles.

"You okay?" Melanie asks. "You look sad."

"I'm fine," I lie, and I think about that word again: *fine*, how it means *okay* but also *thin, light, insubstantial*.

Melanie stands there silently for a moment, then says, "This play is rough, you know. You're allowed to be kind of fucked up about it."

The play is one splinter. I'm pretty sure Melanie's not ready for the whole tree.

"Maybe I am," I say. "Fucked up about it."

"I feel like people don't get this play a lot of the time," Melanie says, making herself comfortable on the floor. "Like, they always call it 'the jealousy play.' But it's not really about jealousy, is it? It's about loss."

I look up at her. "What do you mean?"

"Iago is afraid, right, of losing his wife, his status. So he forces loss on others—makes Othello thinks he's lost Desdemona, which makes him lose his mind. It's this play about grief, but everybody thinks it's about what Iago wants. It's not about what he wants, it's about what he fears. Iago's tragedy is that he lives in fear and makes other people live in fear too."

I pull one of my sleeves over my wrist and the back of my hand, curling the fabric in my fist.

"Makes sense," I say, and it does.

But in so many ways it doesn't.

"The thing is, I don't get why Othello believes Iago," I say. "He's so sleazy."

"What, your friends have never led you astray?" Melanie says. "Carlos, hanging from the bridge? Getting tossed out of fountains?"

It hurts, a little, to hear her say that, like an ache in a strained muscle after you've pushed yourself too hard.

"Yeah, okay," I say. "But he never straight-up lied to me."

The second I say it, I realize I'm not sure if it's true.

"We're a society of pretenders," Melanie murmurs.

"Like Iago," I say.

"Like Othello," Melanie says.

I blink. "You think so?"

"Sure," Melanie says. "Nobody's that smooth. That's why he breaks down in the end, right? Because he can't keep pretending everything's perfect with his perfect wife, can't keep being the perfect soldier and the perfect leader."

"I thought he broke down because he thought his wife was cheating on him with one of his friends," I say.

"Yeah, because it ruins this image he has of her," Melanie says. "Perfect wife isn't so perfect! Gotta kill her."

"That seems kind of—"

"Right?" Melanie says. "It is right, because I am brilliant."

I smile. It sneaks up on me, a surprise pressing at the corners of my mouth, turning them up.

We wander over to the half-finished sets, and I crouch down next to her as she paints over the rough wooden surface with a steady hand. She turns to me, the tightness around her eyes an indicator of her close focus and concentration.

"Nice job," I say.

"I don't know what I'm doing at all," she says.

"You look like you do," I say.

Melanie looks at me with unblinking eyes. "Is that what matters? That I can fake it?"

"You're good at this, Melanie. You are."

"Thanks," she says, but she says *thanks* like I say *fine*, that automatic reply with no truth behind it, no weight.

You are brilliant, I want to say. You are brilliant, Melanie Ellis.

"Go out with me," I say.

Melanie's lips part. "What?"

"You heard me."

"What does that have to do with—"

"Nothing," I cut her off. "Go out with me. For real. Just the two of us."

"Go out with you where?" Melanie asks. She's blushing, and she looks like she's fighting a smile of her own.

"You decide," I say.

• • •

The next day I'm sitting backstage and thumbing through my blocking script when Tristan appears. He collapses next to me and sighs dramatically.

"Solve my problems, Damon Lewis," Tristan says.

"Sure thing," I say, turning a page. "Tell me your problems, and I will solve them."

"There is nowhere that Bryan and I can make out," Tristan says. "His parents are not cool with the gayness, and my parents don't know about the gayness—"

"That sucks," I say. "If it makes you feel any better, my parents don't really approve of me bringing girls home to make out with either."

"People say that teenagers are having a lot of sex these days," Tristan meditates. "But I have no idea how this is possible. Where are these mythical teenagers having all this mythical sex?"

"Clearly backstage at theater rehearsal," I say, wiggling my eyebrows.

"Hey, I did not have sex back here," Tristan says. "We were very rudely interrupted, if I recall."

"I really hope you weren't going to have sex back here. It's gross, man. There are probably rats."

"Who are you making out with, anyway?" Tristan deflects.

Wow, Tristan doesn't miss much.

"Uh," I say. "Nobody?"

"Hey, no, you don't get to . . . Wait, I saw that! There is making out on your horizon, isn't there? Dish, player."

"Melanie didn't—" I start to say, and Tristan clamps his hand down on my wrist.

"Melanie didn't tell me anything," Tristan says, breathless. "But you can tell me everything."

I laugh, extricating my wrist from Tristan's grip. "There's nothing to tell, man."

"Are you going out? Please tell me you're going out."

"Ball's in her court," I say. "I asked her out. Now she just has to say yes."

"Well, Jesus," Tristan says, and yanks his cell phone out of his pants pocket. "We can solve this right now—"

I grasp Tristan's shoulder, stilling him. "Don't do that."

"I just—" Tristan stops. "You're right. I shouldn't pressure her, you shouldn't pressure her, but sometimes Melanie can be really frustrating, you know? You might have noticed she puts up a bit of a front."

"Might have noticed, yeah."

"She doesn't have a lot of experience with boys. I mean— maybe I shouldn't have said that." Tristan exhales loudly. "I'm such a dumbass. I should just shut up—"

"Hey, no," I say. "Relax, Tristan. It's just a date."

"Yeah, well." Tristan tugs a hand through his unruly hair. "What I'm saying is, it's not just a date for Melanie."

My heart trips. I clutch my script more tightly, wrinkling the pages.

That night I get a text from Melanie, short and sweet: ok. location tbd.

I text back: \o/, then do the physical approximation in my bedroom, alone, where no one can see.

A few moments later I get a text that says simply: do u like the blues?

the color palette? I text back.

etta james, she texts. smartass. tribute show at blues alley, this weekend.

My fingers itch, and my heartbeat quickens. A lot of people like Etta James, right, but—I don't think I've ever met anybody my age who likes her the way I do. Punk rock girl wants to take her many piercings and ripped jeans and flaming hair to a blues concert? This is where she most wants to go?

Then again, Etta James is sort of the definition of punk. Talk about a sassy, uncompromising woman.

what time? I text back.

I don't usually get nervous before dates, but come Friday, I'm definitely shaky. I try on a couple outfits—slip on a dressy shirt and slacks, add a jacket, take the jacket off, consider a tie, then mentally kick myself. We're going out to a mid-range restaurant and a club, not the Kennedy Center. I finally settle on something simple, just jeans, a dark blue button-up and black Nikes.

I tap my fingers on the steering wheel to the beat of Otis Redding, groove a little, breathe.

"Hi," she says when I arrive at her front door.

"Hey," I say. "You look beautiful."

She does, in a black skirt and black boots, her shirt made of some slightly shimmery blue fabric. Her eyes are dark, made darker by eyeliner, and her hair hangs in soft waves to her shoulders.

"Thank you," she says.

There's this awkward moment when I hold out my hand to help her down the steps, and she takes it and shakes it, but then I keep holding on because—I can see her processing it—I want to hold her hand. Melanie looks like she's concentrating very hard on the toes of her black boots, but doesn't pull away.

"Let's get going," I say. "That cheesecake ain't gonna eat itself."

The Cheesecake Factory at Chevy Chase Pavilion is crazy crowded, like it always is on a Friday night. Normally we'd have to wait in line for about six hours, but I get us in right away because the hostess remembers me. She's this pretty, light-skinned black girl wearing a low-cut dress that accentuates the curves of her hips and makes her look like a model. She hangs on my arm and laughs all tinkly as she shows us to our table, and I smile back at her. I know exactly what she's doing. Mama didn't raise no fool.

"You look amazing, D," she simpers.

"Do girls always do that?" Melanie asks once we're seated.

"What?" I ask, feigning innocence.

"Throw themselves at you," she says.

I shrug, but I feel a little embarrassed. "Sometimes, I guess."

"I'd never be able to do that," she says. "Just assume that some guy wants me and go for it."

I never thought of it like that. I don't tend to notice when girls do that, maybe because I'm used to Carlos distracting them, flirting—

I clear my throat.

"This place is crazy," I say.

Waiters dressed all in white flutter around carrying plates heaped with mounds of food.

"Everything's pretty good," she says. "I'm just excited to have somebody serve me for a change."

I chuckle. "Yeah, I don't know how you stand waiting tables. I'd get so tired of people."

"Oh, you mean like customers who come in and only order black coffee and nothing else?" she asks, smirking.

"Hey, I tip well. You didn't complain so much when I was there," I say with a sly smile. "I think maybe you like me."

She waves her hand dismissively.

"Yeah, right," she says, then: "Maybe a little."

I shake my head. She tilts her head to the side and winks, big and exaggerated.

The waiter comes and takes our order. We both order pasta: I get fettuccine alfredo, she gets spaghetti with marinara.

"How do you feel like the play is going?" Melanie asks.

I shrug. "All right, I guess. Still hard. But it's a Shakespearean tragedy, not *High School Musical*, so—"

"Hey, those *High School Musical* kids worked really hard," Melanie says seriously, and I snort.

"I like it," I say, "but sometimes I don't want to be there. You know?"

"Sure," she says. "I could never do what you do."

"Well, I couldn't paint a set to save my life," I say.

"What do you think about when you're up there on-stage?" Melanie asks. "I just . . . Watching you guys, I wonder."

"I don't know," I say. "Nothing."

That's a lie. It's more like everything—all my thoughts mash together until they're white noise, a humming background intensity that somehow feeds me energy and anger and grief.

"Nothing?" Melanie says, skeptical. "Really?"

"I think about the character, what the character's feeling," I say. "And it becomes what I'm feeling, I guess."

"That's so weird," Melanie says. "And sort of awesome, too."

"Sometimes it's scary," I say.

I think of Othello and his shaking rage. *'Twas I that killed—*

"Why do it, then?"

"You know that feeling you get when you watch a horror movie and somebody jumps out from behind a door and your whole body tenses up?" I say. "That's the feeling I get onstage. It's the good kind of scary."

Melanie slides one finger down the laminated surface of the table, her forehead creasing.

"It's like falling for somebody," I say, without thinking. "Scary as hell, but worth it."

Melanie glances up, and our eyes meet. She blinks at me, biting her lip.

How can you think you're not one of the pretty girls, Melanie?

"Yeah," Melanie murmurs. "The good kind of scary."

"The best kind," I murmur.

I don't look away, and neither does she.

After dinner we drive over to Georgetown and spend forever finding parking. *C'est la vie.* I don't mind. It gives me more time to look at Melanie up close, to watch the way her eyes shine when she talks about Etta.

"She was just so strong, you know?" Melanie says. "Like— so strong and so tough and so fierce."

I was right. Ain't nobody more punk rock than Etta.

The club is packed and the crowd is mixed, black and white and all shades in between. It's a rare all-ages show, but we're still definitely some of the youngest people there. I mention this to Melanie and she nods, as if it's expected.

"I think a lot of kids our age don't appreciate music that isn't right in front of them," she says. "Like if it's not Top 40, it's not worth listening to."

"We appreciate it, though," I say.

Melanie smiles up at me. "We're special."

The singer who climbs onto the stage is named Chantelle. She doesn't look anything like Etta. She's tall and willowy and dark-skinned, but when she flicks a strand of her short-cropped hair out of her eyes and strikes a pose, my breath quickens. I can already tell she's the real deal.

I've been listening to Etta since I was a little kid, Sunday afternoons with my dad and his jacked-up record player, her voice scratchy from many years of cigarettes and distorted by the well-worn grooves in the vinyl.

The low throb of the guitar pulses through me, the drums a steady snap. Melanie moves her hips to the beat, back and forth, not quite a shimmy. Chantelle implores invisible Henry, all that talk about rolling. Took me a long time to understand what Etta was really singing about.

I touch the inside of Melanie's wrist with my fingers and then hold her hand. We sway like limber tree branches, easy and graceful.

I like Melanie like this: unraveled, boneless, not afraid. She smells like grass after rain. When I place one hand at the small of her back I find she's sweaty there, moisture collecting along her spine. I feel it and I know: I want to touch her. I want to hear the music she makes.

I can hear her telling me something. She shouts over the music but it doesn't quite make it to me.

All I want to do is watch her mouth move.

She angles her chin up and stands on her tiptoes to shout into my ear, "She's beautiful."

And she is—Chantelle is no Etta but she's still gorgeous, slim-hipped and dirty-mouthed with wicked inflection, her voice making all the hairs on my arms stand at attention.

When those familiar violin strings begin, Melanie shifts so she's facing me, and I wrap my arms around her so it's almost like we're dancing. The crowd presses us close.

I lean down. I hear Melanie inhale and the tart sweetness of Chantelle's voice, but mostly I feel the press of Melanie's lips against mine.

She tastes like tomato sauce and mint. She curls her hand in my hair and pulls me closer and I go with her.

I will go where you want to take me, Melanie Ellis.

Melanie

We used to write stories on the ceiling with the glow-in-the-dark stars. You always saw bears—bears having a picnic, bears going to market, bears discovering new planets. I thought this was silly, but now whenever I see stars I think: Ursa Major, Ursa Minor.

I can see your name in your hair, *you said once. You said things like that all the time, things that didn't make sense if you thought about them too much. You were always the artist, always the creative and weird one. Sometimes I didn't want you to be weird, to always be drawing attention to yourself. I wanted you to be like everybody else. I used to get so frustrated, like why couldn't you just be a normal mom who said normal things?*

But now—I see your name in my hair, DANA ELLIS, the way you used to write it, little curlicues on the ends of the letters like children trailing behind. I wonder if I'll always see these things, or if they will fade like my glow-in-the-dark stars. They don't glow anymore. Now, every time I turn out

the lights I think I won't be able to see you, crouch-
ing over my bed in the darkness, pushing your
fingers through my hair. But I do, even without
that soft, hazy light.

CHAPTER SIX

The morning after my date with Damon, my phone rings at the ass crack of dawn.

"Melanie," Tristan says, and I groan. "Wait, don't hang up."

"Jesus Christ, Tristan," I say. "It's, like, oh-dark-thirty."

"I woke up and I couldn't go back to sleep because I kept thinking about your date."

"You're stupid," I say, and grasp blindly for the clock, turning it around so I can read it. "I can't believe you called me at six thirty on a Saturday morning because you wanted to ask me about my date."

"You don't go out on dates often, you know," Tristan says. "It's a special occasion."

"Can I go back to sleep now?"

"No, no, you have to tell me everything."

"Seriously," I say. "You are annoying and I hate you."

"Was it good? At least tell me if it was good."

"It was good. It was very nice. He's a very nice boy."

There's a long-suffering sigh on the other end.

"God. You suck."

"Yeah, I know. Sleeping now."

"Later I expect a complete breakdown with a play-by-play, okay? Just so you know."

"Mmm."

"I'll just be over here, alone and sad. Thinking about where my life went wrong."

"Right."

"Wondering why my best friend won't share the important things in her life with me."

"Uh-huh."

"Imagining a world where people are kind to each other, where—"

"Oh, shut up, Tristan."

Four hours later I wake up for real, stumble down the stairs and putter around the kitchen, making coffee. Dad is probably still asleep—he always works late on Fridays and sleeps in on Saturdays, letting Dahlia handle the brunch crowd. People often assume that having a dad who works in a restaurant would be awesome because I should get good food all the time, but it does not work that way. Usually my dad is too tired to cook, and leftover diner food is gross. American cheese, when melted and cold and congealed, is basically nuclear waste.

"Hey," I hear from behind me, and turn to see Dad standing in the doorway, looking sleepy and rumpled. He scratches at his stubble and blinks. "What time did you get in last night?"

"Uh, like midnight?" I say.

"You were out with Tristan?" He smiles. "I like Tristan. He's a good kid."

"Tristan is a good kid," I say, pouring cereal into a bowl, "but no, I was not out with Tristan. I was out with Damon."

His face falls. "Damon? Who's Damon?"

I take in a breath. "Damon Lewis. He goes to my school. He's in the play, so we've been hanging out."

"And you two were . . ."

I shrug. "I don't know. It's a thing."

"A thing?" He laces his fingers together and cracks his knuckles. "Please describe this thing."

I can see my mom sprawled on my bed, chin in her hands, saying: *He sounds hot.*

I would wrinkle my nose and say, *Ew, Mom, don't be gross.*

"I don't want to talk about it," I say.

You're not her.

You can't be her.

I'm sorry.

He looks defeated, slumped in the doorway in his pajama pants and undershirt, dark hair going gray and thinning at his forehead. For a second he seems old, which is crazy, because he's not even fifty. But you don't have to be old to look old. You don't have to be old to die.

"I have homework," I whisper, dumping my cereal into the sink and pushing past him into the living room.

I think I see wetness on his cheeks as I pass him, but that can't be right. Not my dad. He doesn't do that.

Tristan comes over later that afternoon and proceeds to harass me about Damon and the date in person, just like I knew he would.

"Cheesecake Factory!" Tristan exclaims, bouncing on my bed. "Classiest of establishments."

"Don't make fun," I say. "It's not like your boyfriend is taking you out for a ten-course meal followed by dancing."

"Ugh, don't remind me," Tristan says, flopping down on his back. "Romance is dead."

My phone buzzes with a text.

Damon: `i really enjoyed our evening. so nice to be with someone who understands the awesomeness of the blues. let's do it again soon?`

Tristan snatches my phone away before I can stop him and makes a squawking noise.

"All that and a gentleman too?" he says. "Melanie, you may have found the perfect man. Do you know what the last thing Bryan texted me was?"

He shoves his phone at me. It reads: `ur so good with yr tongue.`

I laugh, and he makes a face.

"Come on, he totally appreciates you," I say. "That's basically poetry."

"The worst," he states. "The *worst*."

"Damon's not perfect either, you know," I say.

"Really?" he says. "Like he picks his nose? His socks don't match? What imperfection does he have that sullies him in your eyes, Ms. Ellis?"

"Hey, I'm not that picky," I say.

Tristan raises his eyebrows. "You kind of are, Melly."

"It's not like I've had a lot of choices," I say, feeling defensive.

"That's a lie," Tristan says. "You just always *think* you don't have a lot of choices."

"When have I had choices?" I ask.

"That guy Ridley last year," Tristan says. "He was nice, and he had that cute haircut, and he liked you a lot."

"He did not!" I say.

"He flirted with you all the time in English," Tristan says. "He kept trying to get you to join Art Club."

"Who wants to be in Art Club?" I say. "Lame."

"Malcolm, your chem lab partner." Tristan ticks off on his fingers. "He was into you sophomore year."

"How was I supposed to know—"

"He did, like, all the work for you on your lab reports," Tristan reminds me.

"I thought he just really liked chemistry," I say, and Tristan actually laughs at me.

"There was that kid from Mexico, what was his name—"

"Pablo, the exchange student," I say. "But that was because I spoke Spanish to him—"

"Do you hear yourself?" Tristan says. "You're making so many excuses! Boys like you sometimes. They do. But you always find some reason that they couldn't like you for real."

Is that true?

You have to let them in, I hear my mom say.

But when you let them in—

Then you have to let them see you.

"I mean, there's nothing wrong with being choosy. Lord

knows sometimes I wish I was a little more . . . well." Tristan sighs. "My choices are more limited."

"Just wait until New York," I say absently.

Tristan brightens. "Yeah," he says. "New York will be the best."

The silence blankets us. I sit very still and try to organize my meandering thoughts.

"Damon, though," Tristan says, finally. "He seems different."

I think of the way he felt pressed against me, his hand at the small of my back. His lips soft on mine.

Safe. He felt safe.

"Yeah," I say. "He does."

I text Damon back: `same. definitely soon.`

Sunday afternoon I'm yawning my way through a particularly deadly passage of *Ethan Frome* when my cell phone begins doing a frantic tap dance on my nightstand. I lean over and grab it, reading the caller ID.

Fag to Hag, it says.

I swipe it open.

"What's up, Tristan?"

There's a short pause, followed by some heavy breathing, then Tristan's voice, sounding too high and faint and far away.

"Melly? Mel?"

I shift the phone from one ear to the other.

"I'm here, hon, what's up?"

"We got problems, Ellis. Big problems."

"What's going on? Where are you?"

"I'm somewhere round Tenley, but I'm heading your direction."

I pause. My dad digs Tristan, but I'm not sure he's ever quite understood our close friendship. This has led to a lot of awkward conversations about why we spend so much time together, and doesn't Tristan have a *girlfriend* he wants to spend time with? In the past that's when Mom would step in and change the subject, smile quirking her lips, eyes reading plain and clear: *You owe me, daughter of mine.*

"Can you tell me what's up? I'm starting to feel a little Twilight Zone here."

"I . . . Mel, it's complicated. Bryan and I were at my house, on the couch, and I told him it was a mistake to be there, but it wasn't . . . we weren't even *doing* anything, just kissing, and then my father came home early and we had the music turned up and—"

The phone cuts out then, but I know how this story goes. I've known since the first time I saw Tristan kiss a boy at a party two years ago, cloaked in darkness and wedged into a corner where no one would be able to tell it wasn't a typical drunken, horny ninth-grade couple hooking up on a Saturday night.

I won't say *I told you so* but I did, I did tell him over and over again—*tell your family the truth*—and now I'm going to help him handle the fallout from not taking my excellent advice, because that's what friends do.

Tristan looks a mess when he arrives on my doorstep,

dark hair tousled and sticking up at odd angles, backpack hastily slung over his shoulder and half-unzipped, dark green polo shirt rumpled. His eyes are red and hazy and heavy with tiredness, and he's got dried blood dotting his lip where it looks like he bit through it.

I let him in and wrap my arms around him in a tight hug, not letting go as his backpack slips off his shoulders and drops to the floor with a thump. Tristan's so tense, I can feel his muscles moving under his skin. We breathe together for a few minutes, matching each other's rhythm until he's not shaking anymore.

"Hot chocolate?" I ask.

He nods. I lead him to the couch and he sits down, staring off into space. I disappear into the kitchen for a few minutes and return carrying two mugs of warm beverage. We sit for another minute sipping in silence before he says, "He's not going to forgive me."

I'm momentarily confused.

"Who? Bryan? Fuck him then."

Tristan turns his sad blue eyes on me. "No. My dad. He's not going to forgive me."

I'm tempted to repeat myself, *Fuck him then*, to brush it off or make a joke, but I know that's not what Tristan needs right now. This is Tristan's family, his blood. He didn't choose them, but he can't just toss them away either.

"You really think—"

"Yes," Tristan says. "I really do. You should have seen the look on his face, Melly, it was like—"

He stops, playing with a loose thread of his jeans.

"He hates me," he says. "And my mom will hate me for being so inconvenient and different, and Jason and Danny will hate me eventually too, because it's not cool in my family to have a brother who's a fag."

"You don't know that," I say.

What else is there to say? Maybe his father won't forgive him. Maybe he is that much of an ass. It's hard to anticipate the extent of a parent's love—or the persistence of their bigotry.

"I just—I always knew what my dad wanted for me, you know? To be the successful one who makes money and marries well and does all the older brother things. He wants me to be the one who shows Jason and Danny how to be men, whatever that means. And I can't do that. Not in the way he wants me to."

I want to tell Tristan that he is a man, that he's more of a man than the many other boys I know—that his sensitivity is a strength, and that the way he loves is a part of what makes him beautiful. I want to tell Tristan's dad that he should be grateful to have a son, grateful he's still around. If he were to lose Tristan, none of this would matter anymore. All that would matter would be the space he left behind.

But this is my damage, not Tristan's. This is who I am now.

"Maybe you can make him understand," I murmur.

Tristan sighs, curling his legs underneath him on the couch. "Yeah. Right."

We watch *Bring It On* and chase the hot chocolate with chocolate ice cream. I sprawl across the couch, head in Tristan's lap, and he runs his hand through my hair idly, smoothing out the tangles. Then he braids sections of it into narrow plaits spliced with red dye like they've been stabbed.

We laugh at how stupid Kirsten Dunst is, and Tristan gets all irate about the injustice of the white girls stealing the black girls' cheers, even though we've seen this movie about forty-seven times. The credits roll at the end of the movie, and Tristan nudges me to sit up. I do so with great reluctance.

"So tell me more about Damon, please," Tristan says. "I want a progress report."

"A progress report?" I repeat. "He's not a target I'm trying to secure."

Tristan raises an eyebrow.

I toss a pillow at him in disgust.

"You think your current angst has gotten you out of the doghouse for that crap you pulled with Mrs. McAvoy?" I say. "You're so wrong."

Tristan gives me a devilish smile. "Pretty sweet, right? I'm a smart kid."

"You're an asshole, is what you mean."

"Seriously, I just got dealt, like, the biggest cockblock of my life. The least you can do is let me live through you."

"Nothing's really happened," I say, even though my brain counters my spoken words with *liar, liar, you lie like a rug.*

"Well, get on that," Tristan says, nudging me with his

shoulder. "You fail as my model of heterosexual behavior if you're not—you know."

"If I'm not behaving heterosexually?"

"If you're not behaving sexually, yes." Tristan nods. "So go, go, Gadget, go."

"What would I do without you?" I sigh.

"Probably die," Tristan says, very seriously.

I elbow him in the ribs, and he pretends he's been mortally injured.

"What does Bryan think about all this?" I ask.

Tristan shrugs.

"I don't know, he basically ran when my dad showed up and freaked."

"Are you going to talk to him?" I say.

Tristan's eyes lose their blue luster.

"Yeah," Tristan says. "If he wants to talk about it."

"He's as much a part of this as you are—"

"I know, Mel. I know," Tristan says. "I'm sorry about all this. Showing up, being a drama queen. I didn't mean to—"

"Tristan, it's okay," I say. "I'm your BFF, remember? This is what I do."

He sighs, shoulders slumping. Tristan's not a big guy, and he looks even smaller right now, deflated like a beach ball that's been left out in the backyard too long.

"You remember back in third grade, when we broke your mother's favorite vase because we were reenacting scenes from *Star Wars*?" I ask. "And you were wigging out, and I said you had to tell her because she was going to find out anyway, and you told her and she yelled at you but afterward she was okay with it?"

Tristan looks at me with tired eyes.

"Melanie, this is not a vase I broke."

"I know, but—" I stop.

Tristan is hugging his knees. His brow wrinkles in concentration.

"What does your dad want you to do?" I ask.

"Be less gay?" he postulates. "I don't know, Mel. He's a dick, and my mother's not much better. I thought she might at least take my side, but she's so afraid of him that she just sits by and lets him get away with saying all this shit, and Danny and Jason are so confused, and I feel like—"

He stops, shaking his head. He's run out of words.

I sigh, letting my hand fall to cup the back of Tristan's neck. His skin is soft under my palm, slightly moist with sweat.

"They're going to let you stay, right?" I ask. "They're not kicking you out or anything."

Tristan shakes his head.

"They'll let me stay. Not that I want to stay, but yeah. They're not totally awful."

I wish I could tell Tristan, *Stay with me, I will let you stay for as long as you want,* but I know if I do I'll just be letting Tristan's parents win, letting them get rid of him and his complications.

"You'll be okay," I whisper, pressing my thumb into the nape of his neck.

I think about my mom, and my dad, and Tristan and Bryan and Tristan's parents. I think about Damon and the way his eyes go dark whenever he talks about Carlos, like someone inside him flicked off the light.

I think of that sketchbook under my bed.

I think about secrets, and keeping them, and how long a person can do that before it starts to eat them up inside. How long before they start wishing they could shout it from the rooftops or carve it into someone's skin.

I curl my hand into a fist, nails prickling my palm.

Over the next week, my days become a blur of school, play rehearsal, working, sleeping and eating. School is boring and work is boring, but play rehearsal? Play rehearsal has its perks.

The actual painting of sets is pretty tedious, though there is a Zen element to it that I dig. It's very repetitive and physical, slicking the paint over wood or sanding things with that back-and-forth friction motion, but at the end of the rehearsal I can look at what I've done and see it in front of me, this product I've created. It's weirdly gratifying in an *oh wow, I made that* sort of way, similar to the satisfaction I got as a kid when I made ugly paintings out of macaroni or built leaning houses from Popsicle sticks.

There's Max too, short for Maxine, who joined the set-building crew a week or so after me. Max is cool. She wants to be a comic book artist when she's older, and she's got fabric patches with drawings of superheroes stitched all over her backpack. Some are just your standard superheroes, Batman and Spider-Man and the Hulk, but some are super-heroes she created, like this one called the Haberdasher, who dresses in a pinstripe suit and wears really sweet hats.

"His hats are made of this ultra-sharp material that can cut through skin," Max explains. "So he throws them at people and slices them in half."

"Like that guy in the Bond movies," I say. "Oddjob."

"Yeah, like him, but awesomer," Max says.

"How would it be awesomer?" Calvin asks, sounding pained. "It's exactly the same."

"It just would be," Max replies, and there's really nothing Calvin can say to that.

I'm crouched down, painting the castle walls onto can-vas, gray and looming against a dark night sky.

Max nods, appreciative.

"Nice work, Melanie."

"Thanks," I say, smiling. I bite back the desire to say something self-deprecating. I want to ask Max how it's so easy for her, to draw and paint and not worry about what people think.

But I don't.

Damon wanders backstage while I'm painting and stands around watching for a few minutes before I say, "It's a pretty bitchin' castle, isn't it?"

I can feel Damon smile behind me. "It is. Those turrets are hot."

"You ever want to live in a castle? Like as a kid?" I ask, and

Damon kneels down, resting his hand on my shoulder and keeping it there. I can feel the heat through my shirt.

"Not really," Damon says. "Castles seem like they'd be cold. And damp. And hard to keep clean."

I laugh. "I guess so. But you could have, like, drawbridges and shit. That'd be kind of sweet."

"Mmm," Damon murmurs.

He reaches out and holds his hand over the painting, not touching it, just hovering. When I look at him, questioning, he says, "Carlos used to do this sometimes when we'd go on field trips to art museums. He said he could feel vibes or something. Like he could feel what the artist was feeling when they were painting it."

I stare at Damon. He's not looking at me, his eyes trained on the set piece, brow furrowed.

"That's pretty freaky."

"Yeah," Damon says softly.

"You feel anything?"

"I feel that the person who made this is really talented," Damon says. "And has no idea how talented she is."

I flush. "You're so full of—"

"No," Damon says, and he's looking at me with that straight-on green gaze. "I'm not, Melanie."

I don't say anything, and he finally looks away.

I can hear the murmur of the cast rehearsing nearby, but somehow it feels like Damon and I are the only two people here.

"I think they'd be lonely," Damon says.

I blink. "What?"

"Castles," Damon says. "I think they'd be lonely. Big and dark and empty and lonely."

"Even if you had courtiers and maidens and knights?" I say.

"Yeah," Damon says. "Even then."

The grief book is staring at me when I walk into my bedroom that night. I flip it open, thinking: *Tell me how to feel her close to me.*

> *Are you enjoying your life? This is a question you should be asking yourself, and often. If the answer is yes, this is good. You should not feel bad for enjoying yourself. Living with grief means precisely that: living. You do no service to yourself or the person you are grieving for by acting like you are dead too.*

I flip to another page and read.

> *You need, at some point, to learn to love your grief, to make friends with it, because it will be with you a long time. It is a part of you now.*

Enjoy your life. Love your grief. This book makes it sound like it's just a big old party when someone dies.

I put on my flannel pajamas with ice-skating penguins all over them and climb under the covers and pull the sheets up to my chin. I lie back on my bed and spread out my arms so my fingertips come to the edge of my mattress. The ceiling is a powdery white, seemingly pristine, but I think I see a tiny crack in one corner. It makes me smile to see that even the almost-perfect ceiling is flawed. Everything is a little fucked up, and that's okay.

I flick off my bedroom lamp, but every time I close my eyes I see empty castle hallways, dark and dank and filled with shadows.

"You're there, aren't you?" I say softly. "You're there, and you think I'm being stupid."

I sigh.

"The grief book says you have to love your grief," I say. "But that's some bullshit, right? How can you love your grief? That's dumb."

I grasp a corner of the sheet between my thumb and forefinger, rubbing it against my skin. The sheets are soft, worn thin by many washes. I remember the day my mom taught me how to do laundry. *Whites separate from colors,* she told me, tossing a pair of underwear into one pile, a pair of jeans into another. *Whites get warm water. Colors get cold. If you put colors in warm water they might run.*

Run where? I joked, and Mom made a face at me.

"How do you know who you should let into your life?" I ask. "Do you just decide? Like, should I trust Damon because he's nice to me, and he seems like he's honest?"

What I don't say: *What if I let him in? What if I let him in and I care about him and then I lose him?*

What if I lose him like I lost you?

I flip over on my bed, nestling my head in the pillow.

"I think you'd tell me to wait and see. Wait and see what Damon does, and if he's a good guy then . . . then I'll know. That's what you'd say."

I take in a deep breath, then exhale, slowly, feeling the air fill and leave my lungs.

"Am I stupid, Mom? Can you just tell me that?"

No answer.

I tug on my pajama sleeve, sighing. I lift my hand to my cheek. It's wet. When did I start crying? I turn to one side, blotting my cheek on the pillow. What the hell am I crying for?

You lost your mother, the voice inside my head reminds me. *That's not supposed to happen. It's not supposed to happen to anyone, ever, but it does, and it sucks, and there's nothing you can do about it.*

I flop over on my back, curling my hands into fists.

"He likes me," I say. "I think he really likes me, Mom."

Sunday night about mid-shift, Macho hands me a plate holding a cheeseburger and fries for table five and gives me a big wink. I shoot him a confused look and he says, "We gotta talk, girl," in a tone that fills me with foreboding.

The slightly rumpled older gentleman at table three gives me a filthy smile that makes me shudder. The day I do not have to wait tables ever again will be a glorious one indeed.

"You look like the cat that ate the canary," I say to Macho when I return to the kitchen with an armful of dirty dishes.

"I heard you got a boyfriend," he says in a singsong voice. "How come you don't tell me these things, Mel? I thought we were buds."

I roll my eyes, dumping the plates into a bucket of milky-colored dishwater.

"There's nothing to tell."

This is mostly true. It hasn't been that long since we went on that date, even if it feels like—

My lips burn a little, and I unconsciously lift my hand, stopping myself before I actually touch my mouth.

I am not that kind of girl, Jesus.

But when I nearly lose my grip on dinner for table four, I wonder if maybe I sort of am.

The next morning I wake up too early, even for a school day, and can't get back to sleep. Tired and irritable, I dress slowly and without paying much attention. I'm too lazy to put on my belly chain or find a cute belt, so I pick my leather jacket up off the floor near the hamper, grab my backpack and barely make the bus.

At lunchtime Damon sidelines me in the cafeteria, stepping into my path as I'm on my way to the table where I usually eat with Tristan.

"Is that an order?" Damon asks, eyes flicking down to the text on my T-shirt and then back up at my face.

I'm wearing a red T-shirt bearing a picture of Elmo and the words *Tickle Me* in big black letters.

"Stop staring at my boobs, Lewis," I drawl, and Damon's

smirk makes me want to push him down in the middle of this cafeteria and do unspeakable things to him.

He makes a point of looking me directly in the eye when he says, "Want to come over tomorrow? We could study."

I can practically see the air quotes around the word *study*, but I don't care.

Yeah, I want to come over. I want to "study" with Damon Lewis.

I'm nodding off in U.S. history when my cell phone buzzes at my hip. I shift in my seat, trying not to call attention to myself. Cell phones are expressly forbidden in class. I turn it over in my lap, reading the message: `status report on mr. lewis?`

I fire off a quick reply: `talk later. target secured.`

About thirty seconds pass, then another message: `!!!!!!!!!`

I smile.

That night my dad and I are discussing dinner, specifically how many tomatoes are required to make the sauce rich enough, when he starts in: a stealth attack.

"Here's the thing," he says. "You're my baby girl. Don't look at me like that, Melly. You are. You're my baby girl, and I love you, but that doesn't mean you get to shut me out."

I start to say something, but he bulldozes over me, talking faster.

"I know your mother and I haven't always been hardcore

disciplinarians, but that's because we trusted you. We thought you could handle yourself. I still think you can handle yourself, so don't prove us wrong, please. Trusting you does not make me a lazy father. It may not make me a good father, but I am still your father. And that's . . ." He sighs, running a hand through his thinning hair. "That's what I have to say about that."

There's a few moments of tense silence, and then I clear my throat.

"Um. Dad. A couple of things, if this is honesty time or whatever. First, Tristan is gay. Very, very gay. His parents just found out, and so we've been dealing with that drama. Also, I really like Damon, and I think we might be . . . something. He's a nice guy, and smart, and funny, so . . . yeah."

He stares at me for a moment. He opens his mouth to say something, then closes it, then opens it again.

"Tristan is gay?"

I start laughing.

"No, seriously, he's gay? That—that makes a lot of sense, actually," he says. He scratches his temple, brow furrowing.

I'm still laughing.

"You do realize this means you're going to have to let me meet Damon," he says.

I stop laughing.

"I'm not kidding. You can't date some guy who I haven't had a chance to rake over the coals first," he says, but his eyes are soft and gentle.

"I don't know if I would call it dating."

"What would you call it then?"

There are so many ways to answer that question, and none are dad-proof. All involve words like *casual* and phrases like *friends with benefits*, and Gary Ellis does not like words like these. Mom wouldn't blink, but Dad—

"We're taking it slow," I say.

This sounds good. It sounds chaste and righteous, like a role-play in an abstinence-only sex ed class.

He examines me with his dark eyes. "Slow."

"Yeah," I say.

"But there is something to be taken slow," he says. "There is a relationship that's evolving."

I hear "evolving." I think: *Over the bra. Under the bra.* I consider the bases, and how they almost always seem to be changing, except for going all the way round. No one ever contests what a home run is. No one ever says: *Intercourse, hah, that was all the way back in the '80s, where have you been?*

"It's a relationship, yes," I say. "We just don't know what kind yet."

He gives me a look that seems to indicate his displeasure with my evasiveness, but that is just too bad. I am fully committed to ambiguity. I want to marry it and have its vague, indistinct babies.

"Well, if you need to talk about . . ."

I do not want to have this talk now. It was bad enough the first time around. I remember how Mom sat me down in my bedroom, clasped my hands between hers and said:

148

You have to protect yourself, Mel. No one else is going to do it for you when the time comes.

I glanced down at the bedspread—it was a bright, sunflower yellow, smooth and soft. New. Out of the corner of my eye I could see my teddy bear, Lucy. One of her ears was tattered, a button missing from her shiny green raincoat. My stomach hurt.

My mother had pressed a small, square foil wrapper into my palm. I could feel the sweat collect on my skin under and around it, making it slip between my fingers.

Your dad thinks you're too young for this, she said. *I don't know, sweetheart. I hope . . . I just want you to be prepared.*

I was thirteen. Boys—or at least the boys I knew—were awful. I thought: *Prepared for what?*

"I'm good. Really," I say.

He looks relieved. "Okay. If you have questions, you just let me know."

I smile, leaning forward and patting him on the cheek.

"I love you, Dad."

He grasps my shoulder and squeezes. "I love you too, baby doll."

He goes back to stirring the sauce, and I begin to set the table.

He's humming softly. Sounds like the Beach Boys. The kitchen smells like garlic and pepper and sweet tangy tomatoes. Feels like old times. When I was little, before Dad bought the restaurant and mostly stopped cooking at home, he used to spend Sunday afternoons teaching me how to cook: simple dishes, basic sauces, sautés, burgers, roasts. One October Sunday he showed me how to make tomato sauce from scratch.

At the time, Dad was an accountant, but he loved food more than he would ever love numbers. Our kitchen was a testament to that fact: It was elegant and huge and sun-filled, equipped with all the best fixtures and appliances, and containing a permanently well-stocked fridge. Of all the people I knew, my father was the only one who owned grill pans in different sizes, cake tins for making layer cakes, an egg timer and a pastry brush and six spatulas. This was how my dad operated—be prepared or be sorry.

Clad in ratty sweatpants and slippers and a T-shirt left over from my days as a Girl Scout (I only lasted one year; I was super not into all the nature and group bonding), I helped him sprinkle chopped garlic and onions into a pan sizzling with olive oil. The pungent aroma filled the room. Next came peppers, green and red, seeded and slivered, and more spices—oregano and chopped fresh basil and thyme. Finally there were the tomatoes, diced and bleeding juice all over the white plastic cutting board. I know a lot of kids don't like them, but I always loved tomatoes, especially the ones my father grew in our backyard. I thought they tasted like the sunshine that ripened them, and eating them felt like breathing in sky.

I laughed as I let the tomatoes slither out of my hands and into the crackling oil and spice mixture. Dad dumped in his share as well, telling me: *You want the onions to almost melt, like they're barely there, so you can only taste what's been left behind.* I nodded and helped him stir, swirling crimson liquid going round and round, bubbling, bubbling.

I can still make a mean tomato sauce, but what remains vivid in my mind are his words. *Taste only what's been left behind.* When I think of my mother, I taste rich chocolate from brownies made late on Friday nights in cake pans, salt from movie theater popcorn, sugary coffee, milky sweet ice cream.

When I think of my father, I taste tomatoes.

From here I can see the chip in the kitchen table where I ran my tricycle into it when I was five. There's a spot on the wall in my bedroom where Mom measured my height until I was ten, little pencil marks slowly disappearing into the paint. Dad shifts the pan on the stove and I remember Mom burning herself on it once, yelping and cursing in the kitchen, running it under cold water as Dad said, *Jesus, Dana, you're not dying.*

You're not dying.

This whole house is like that: places everywhere that I can run my hands over the memories. Everyone who touches you leaves their fingerprints—a vestige, a leftover, a mark. My mother's fingerprints are all over me, pressed in so deep, I can see the whorls. And everywhere I look, there they are, as dark as if she etched them in ink.

DAMON

A secret:
Sometimes I want to forget you.

CHAPTER SEVEN

W hat? No, give me that back."
Melanie digs her elbow into my chest,
trying to wrestle away the remote control.
I laugh and hold it up above her head, using my other hand
to pin her against the couch. She makes angry growling
sounds, followed by a string of curses. I laugh harder.

"We are not watching—this—shit—"

She struggles, finally freeing herself from my grip, and
grabs the remote control. I grunt, rolling over on top of her,
still laughing.

Suddenly we are very close. I can feel Melanie's breath
on my face, and her hand clutches at my hip, just above the
waistband of my pants.

"We can watch whatever you want," I say. "*Project Run-
way*? I know you secretly want—"

"Oh, shut up, asshole," Melanie says, digging her fingers into
my arm until I wince. She's got a hell of a grip for a girl. For a
person. "Is this how you study? You must get excellent grades."

"Hey, D, can you take your stuff out of the dry—"

Melanie and I freeze. My mom stands in the doorway of
the living room, one hand on her hip.

"Mom." I unfold myself so I'm no longer on top of
Melanie, who's looking flushed and embarrassed. "This is
Melanie. Melanie, this is my mom."

"Hello, Melanie," my mom says, smiling, and holds out her hand. "It's nice to finally meet you."

"Nice to meet you too," Melanie says, though she mostly looks like she wants to hide under the floor.

"I'll take care of the laundry," I say to my mom.

"Terrible too," she says. "He hasn't been walked today, and you know how he gets when he's inside for too long. I know you love those new Nikes you bought, so unless you want him to tear them up—"

"Yeah, I'll walk him, don't worry about it," I say.

She raises her eyebrows.

"I will, Mom, I swear."

"Okay then," she says, gives me a *we'll talk about this more later* look, and leaves.

There's a moment of silence. Melanie's sitting so still, she's barely breathing.

"Well," she says.

"I'm sorry about that," I say. "I didn't even know she was home yet."

Melanie looks at me, and with a completely straight face says, "Your mom must think I'm some kind of hussy."

I laugh. "Yes, I'm sure that's exactly what she thinks. 'That Melanie, what a strumpet!'"

"That could not have looked good, you on top of me like that—"

"It's okay," I say. "I'm pretty sure my parents would be happy to see me bring home any new friends from school."

"Friend, huh?" Melanie says, poking me in the ribs. "Is this how you treat all your friends?"

I grasp her hand and pull her forward. My hands are large enough to cover hers completely. I can see her breathe, her shoulders rising and falling in waves.

"Only the cute ones," I murmur.

I kiss her, a gentle brush of the lips that quickly becomes something more. Soon I'm dizzy and hot, my fingers gripping hers hard.

"Um, Damon?" Melanie pipes up as we separate for air. "If we don't stop, your mom is going to find us in a way worse position than she did before. I'm just saying."

I take a deep breath and let go of her hand. "You're probably right about that."

We sit in awkward silence for a moment before Melanie says, "So . . . who is Terrible?"

I smile.

"I'll introduce you," I say.

Outside it's a perfect fall day: bright and sunny, air crisp and the tiniest bit chilly. I love this time of year. Pumpkins decorate the front porches of the houses around the neighborhood, wisps of fake cobwebs cling to windows, and plastic skeletons and giant spiders made out of black felt hang above doorways. One family has four pumpkin-headed figures dressed up to look like characters from *The Wizard of Oz*—the Scarecrow, the Tin Man, the Cowardly Lion and Dorothy—perched on the roof of their house.

Terrible, our large, bouncy black Labrador, tugs Melanie along, pulling in the direction of the street, then stops to sniff at an apparently delectable pile of leaves.

"I can't believe you named your dog Terrible," she says.

"And that was before we even knew anything about him," I say with a smirk. "Might have been a bit of a self-fulfilling prophecy."

"You're so weird."

"Thought we'd already established that," I say, pivoting on my heel and walking backward like a tour guide, grinning.

"I think I need to know more about you," Melanie says. "Strange things. Potential blackmail material."

"Really?" I say. "You think we're already at the potential blackmail stage?"

Melanie shrugs. "It's never too early."

"Hmm. I don't know. There aren't any bad things about me."

Terrible barks as if to say, *Yeah, right, whatever.*

Melanie raises an eyebrow.

"I like Queen," I say. "You know, the band Queen?"

"Yes, I know the band Queen," Melanie says. "That's a lame secret. I like Queen too. A lot of people like Queen. Half the world likes Queen. Possibly more than half. They play Queen at every baseball game."

"When I was younger I bought a Nick Jonas and the Administration album," I say. "I told the guy at the store it was for my sister, but I don't have a sister."

"What about his more recent stuff?" she asks, eyes comically wide.

I make an ambivalent motion with my hand. "Not the same. Not the same heart."

She laughs, twisting the leash around her wrist.

We wait at an intersection with a light. Terrible strains against his leash as if he wants to sprint across without her. She yanks backward, keeping him on the sidewalk, and Terrible gives her a look of solemn reproach.

"I played Little League for a while," I say. "I was really bad at it. I'm not that good at basketball either."

"But you hang out with all the—"

"They only hang with me sometimes because Prague and I are cousins," I say. "And they let me know I suck. Often."

Melanie snorts. We come to a small patch of green that claims to be a park and find a bench to sit on. I let Terrible off the leash and he races off across the grass, barking loudly and frantically at invisible ghosts.

"You transferred to Hamilton in your junior year," Melanie says. "That's kind of unusual."

I stiffen. "Yeah."

"You're not going to tell me why?"

"It wasn't working out at Gate," I say.

Melanie looks confused, but she lets it go.

"Carlos and I used to walk Terrible sometimes," I say suddenly. "Carlos didn't like dogs much. He thought they were kind of a pain in the ass, but he liked Terrible. He said he had . . . I don't know, fire in him."

Terrible comes rushing toward us, pivoting at the last second and taking off again, yapping away.

"He's got something in him, that's for sure," Melanie says.

I shake my head, rueful. A siren sounds in the distance.

"I think sometimes that—this is going to sound weird, but do you ever get this feeling like your mom's still around?" I say, turning toward Melanie. "I don't mean that in a delusional way—I mean, I know Carlos isn't around. But sometimes it feels like he's . . . watching. Like he knows what's going on and wants to be a part of it. You know?"

Melanie bows her head, and I can see tension settling across her shoulders like a cape. She's playing with her hands in her lap, folding them together, breaking them apart.

"Yeah," Melanie says. "When I'm painting sets. I think she would've . . . if she was still around, she would have stopped by school to check in on me, to see how things were coming along. She would've been surprised that I was doing it, but she would've been happy."

"I realize I didn't know her," I say, "but I think she would've been happy too."

Melanie reaches out, placing a hand on the small of my back. My spine tingles, buzzing from the base of my spine up to my neck. I imagine for a moment my brain sending messages to the rest of my body from my nerve center, a thousand little rolled-up pieces of paper traveling through my bloodstream to a thousand different destinations, and all of them say the same thing:

I feel you. I feel you.

"What would he say?" Melanie asks. "If he were here right now, what would Carlos say?"

I tilt up my chin, feeling the sun on my skin, cutting through the chilly air.

"I don't know," I say.

"I think maybe you do," Melanie says.

Her insistence surprises me. I feel her fingers curl in my coat, and she doesn't pull her hand away.

"He'd like you," I say. "He'd probably say you've got fire in you too."

"You mean like your dog?" Melanie says.

"Well, you know, man's best friend . . ." I say, and I know the punch I get in the arm is exactly what I deserve.

When our laughter subsides, we sit in silence, my arm aching. I watch Melanie flip her hair out of her eyes. Her eyelashes flicker against her cheeks like a camera shutter.

I want to take her picture.

"Do you think your mom would like me?" I ask.

When I try to meet her eyes, Melanie is looking away. The sun is sinking lower in the sky, the light less glaring, soft-focus.

"Yeah," she says. "She would."

Melanie claims she has to go do actual homework, but I make her promise to come over for dinner the next day. I know she says yes because she can't think of a reason to say no. I imagine many of her meals these days are taken alone since her dad's working at the diner so much, left-overs heated through in the microwave and eaten in front of the TV, or occasionally at the restaurant at the metal tables in the kitchen, trying to stay out of the way of the line cooks as they holler orders and clang their pots and pans. One place is quiet, the other is noisy, but both seem lonely. There's no looking across the table and catching someone's eye and thinking, *Yes, we are in this moment and here we are.*

This, Melanie, I can do for you.

My mom greets Melanie with a warm smile when she arrives home, saying, "Oh, good, we can chat! Yesterday Damon spirited you away before we got acquainted."

I raise an eyebrow. I've told my parents very little about Melanie. I don't talk to my parents much anymore. I don't know what to say.

Melanie looks terrified, but my mom simply laughs and pats Melanie on the arm, saying, "It's okay, honey. I promise you won't feel a thing."

We stand around the kitchen while she pieces together a simple meal of lemon chicken and rice and string beans. Melanie suggests adding a pinch of dill to the marinade and then backtracks, saying, "I'm sorry, my dad's a chef. I think I inherited his habit of backseat cooking."

"Never apologize for helping to create something, Melanie," Mom says.

Melanie looks down at her shoes, black motorcycle boots with silver buckles and chunky heels, and says nothing. I rest a hand on her shoulder until she looks up at me and shares my smile.

"So what are your favorite classes?" Mom asks her when we're all seated around the table and digging in.

"Um, I like English," she says.

"You like to read?" my father asks. He's wearing his wire-rim glasses perched precariously on the edge of his nose, and he leans forward as he speaks. "Maybe some of that will rub off on Damon. He's only ever interested in this acting stuff, but I keep telling him that reading is important too—"

"I read," I cut in. "I do, Dad."

"The backs of cereal boxes, maybe," he jokes, but a smile pushes at his lips.

"What do you like to do outside of school?" Mom asks. "Any extracurriculars?"

"Mom," I say, a warning.

"I'm sorry for the inquisition," she says, though she doesn't seem all that sorry. "I'm just curious."

"I'm working on painting sets for the play," Melanie says.

"Is that how you met Damon?" Mom says.

Melanie catches my eye, then nods.

Ah, I see Melanie's not so bad at lies of omission either.

"Do you like art? Painting?"

Melanie hesitates. "I do, yeah," she says.

"That's wonderful," my mother says. "The world always needs more artists."

Especially because it's lost one.

"It does," Melanie murmurs, and I watch her bask in my mom's wide smile.

I don't know what Melanie's mother looked like, but I can imagine her, paint-splattered and laughing, gesturing at Melanie with a brush tipped with red. *Now you try it*, I see her saying, pushing a stack of thick paper over to Melanie. *Now you.*

After Melanie's gone, I poke my head into my father's study to say, "I took out the trash."

"Thank you," Dad says, adjusting his glasses so he can peer over them. "Are you okay?"

"I'm fine," I say, automatic.

My parents do this now: constant check-ins.

"Melanie seems sweet."

I can't think of a worse word to describe Melanie than *sweet*, except maybe *perky*.

"Melanie's great," I say. "I really like her."

"I'm glad you're making friends at Hamilton," Dad says. "That's a good step."

Step toward what? But I know—a step toward moving on, moving away. A step toward thinking about Carlos less, letting him fade. Replacing him. Filling up the space.

But Melanie will never fill up that space. She fills a different space that is Melanie-shaped, a space I didn't even realize I needed to fill until she appeared in my life. It doesn't make sense to expect her to fill the Carlos space, the one shaped like our inside jokes and shoving matches, like Halo battles on Saturday afternoons, like late-night conversations about serious shit we couldn't talk about in daylight.

Nobody will ever fill that space, and now I must learn to build around it, to insulate it with distance. These are the bricks and mortar of grief, the worst kind of construction. You never build anything beautiful. You just caulk the cracks and hope nothing crumbles.

I stop by the restaurant a few days later after play practice when Melanie's working and settle in at my usual table. She brings me coffee and gives me a small smile.

"Terrible ate one of my Nikes this morning," I lament. "He gutted it, man. There were little pieces of shoelaces all over my room."

"Did you forget to walk him?" Melanie asks.

"Oh my God," I say, rolling my eyes. "I only need one mother."

"Sneaker death." Melanie nods, sympathetic. "The most tragic."

"It is tragic," I say, stirring my coffee. "I was thinking of burying them in the backyard, but my dad says that's not good for the environment. Something about Nikes not being compostable."

"You could put up a headstone," Melanie suggests. "Something decorative and subtle. 'Here lies one tennis shoe, destroyed in its prime by a wild animal . . .'"

"'It will be missed,'" I continue. "'It is survived by its close friends, Air Jordans and Vans.'"

Someone clears his throat behind us. I peer around Melanie, curious.

A tall, dark-haired man with a slightly receding hairline stands there. He gives me a careful smile. "Hello. I'm Gary."

I'm slightly confused. "Hi, Gary."

He takes my hand and shakes it. He raises his eyebrows. "I own this place," he says. "You know. Gary's."

I nod, and then realization dawns on me. "Gary. Right. Good to meet you, sir."

Nice save.

"I understand that you and my daughter have a thing," Melanie's dad says, and Melanie cringes.

"A thing?" I say. Possibly my voice cracks a little.

"This is what she calls it," Gary says. "Melanie's always been good with words."

"That's why I like her, sir," I say. "She's so articulate."

Gary throws his head back and laughs, and Melanie looks like she doesn't know who she wants to smack first, him or me.

"You're both bastards," Melanie mutters. "I have to work."

"I want you to come to dinner sometime, Damon," Gary says. "Not at the restaurant. I'll make something you could never get at a diner. Something French."

"That sounds amazing, sir," I say. "I would love that."

Melanie's expression is a mixture of frightened and annoyed. As she turns to leave, I reach out and catch her by the arm, saying, "Hey, Mel, is this going to affect our 'thing'?"

Melanie shoots me a look that could've killed Rasputin.

"Friday," I say. "Are you busy?"

I give her my best smile.

"Why," she deadpans. "You want to hang out with my dad, since the two of you are getting along so well?"

"I'd rather hang out with you," I say.

I can see her wavering.

"Come on," I say. "It'll be awesome. You know it will."

"Okay," she says. "But it better be fabulous."

I grin into my coffee as she walks away.

I leave the restaurant feeling light on my feet, but the more space I put between myself and Melanie, the heavier my feet become. The week ahead skims through my mind, and my mood quickly fades and sours.

Soon we're going to begin rehearsing the final acts of the play. I plan to go in with my game face on, but I'm not looking forward to it: the rapid disintegration of Othello's sanity, the way his anger grows with each line, the torturous, inevitable fall.

Lacey Andrews is a striking Desdemona with her long, blond hair and flirtatious smile. She plays Desdemona as a simple young girl who's infatuated with Othello but doesn't truly understand him. Every time we do our final scenes, her look of surprise when Othello's deep love shifts to confused hatred feels like pinpricks under my fingernails.

Sometimes I wonder, *Why am I doing this? Why?* Why do I put myself through this, make myself experience these horrible things that aren't even real?

But it feels real. It feels real and wrong and terrible—the betrayal, the anger, the grief. As real as anything feels these days.

And I need it. I need all the moments that feel real to make up for all the ones that don't.

It doesn't help my generally shitty mood that I run into Prague on Wednesday just before play rehearsal for the first time in weeks. I'm about to give him a quick nod of acknowledgment and sprint away, but dammit if my cousin doesn't keep walking toward me.

"'Sup," Prague says. "You got a minute?"

My stomach drops. The look on Prague's face is no joke.

"Uh—I got rehearsal—"

"One minute," Prague promises, and tugs me into the boys' bathroom.

"Everything okay?" I ask.

"You tell me," Prague says. "I hear you got a girlfriend."

I shrug. "I don't know, we haven't exactly given it a label or whatever—"

"Look, I'm not trying to get up in your business," Prague says.

"Sounds like that's exactly what you're trying to do," I retort.

Prague crosses his arms. "I just—I think maybe you don't know about how this works, you coming from a private school and all."

I lift an eyebrow. "How what works, Sam?"

Prague tenses at the use of his real name. "Dating white girls."

"What, is there some kind of handbook? A how-to guide?"

"Don't be a dick, D. I'm trying to tell you—"

"I don't know if I need dating advice from you, man. No offense."

"I'm just saying—people do it, it's not that it's wrong or anything, but you're new here and it looks like you don't like your own kind, D, that's all I'm—"

"I think Melanie is my kind," I say. "What, are you telling me you aren't thrilled to see I'm dating a girl? In the future, you want me to run my choices by you first? You need to screen each girl before I decide to get with her?"

Prague's eyes are dark.

"I'm not trying to be an asshole, yo. I'm telling you how it is."

"Maybe you don't know how it is," I snap.

Prague puts his hands up in a gesture of surrender. "Never mind, then. Forget I said anything."

"I will," I say.

I slam out of the bathroom, face hot. I clench my hands into fists and unfurl them slowly. *How dare you*, I think, but I'm not brave enough to turn around and finish that conversation the way I want to finish it. *It looks like you don't like your own kind?* Jesus Christ.

It's lucky we're rehearsing one of Othello's rage-filled scenes today, because moments later I find myself standing onstage, body tight with fury as I face Lacey-as-Desdemona.

"Heaven truly knows that thou art false as hell," I spit.

"To whom, my lord? With whom?" Lacey gasps. "How am I false?"

"Ah, Desdemona, away, away, away!" I shout.

"I hope my noble lord esteems me honest," Lacey whispers.

"Oh, ay, as summer flies are in the shambles, that quicken even with blowing! O thou weed," I hiss, "who art so lovely fair and smell'st so sweet that the sense aches at thee, would thou hadst ne'er been born!"

"Alas," Lacey says with wide, frightened blue eyes, "what ignorant sin have I committed?"

I falter.

What ignorant—what ignorant sin—

Fuck you, man, I hear Carlos say.

The anger shivers up my vertebrae, unwelcome electricity.

I can see Carlos sprawled against that tree, head lolling to one side, eyes fluttering shut.

Stay with me, stay with me—

I can see Carlos, hunched over and fighting tears on that fire escape as we tried to talk over the shouting going on inside. Carlos's hands shook. Our voices rose until our throats were raw. I imagined passersby puzzling over why these two boys were yelling about Halo, why we were so passionate about *Lord of the Rings* or *Star Wars*, but all I could do was watch Carlos's lips move, forcing myself to block out the sounds of "Bitch, you can't even take care of your own kids right, why should I give you anything?" and "José, you don't know nothing about these kids, you don't know—"

What ignorant sin—

I tried to help. I tried to distract Carlos, to give him things to think about other than his messed-up family. I listened whenever Carlos wanted to talk—well, I tried to listen, but Carlos didn't talk much about that stuff. He never wanted to, and how could I make him talk about what he didn't want to talk about?

I tried to be a good friend, tried to be there, and still, still, whatever I did, it didn't matter.

In the end it was Carlos who made that decision, Carlos who—

What ignorant sin—

I could have stopped it. There were so many times— there were so many things—

What ignorant sin—

The words run together in my mind and separate out and trip over each other, jerking and repeating like samples in a hip-hop song. I back up, putting out one hand as if to shield myself, and stumble.

"Damon?" Lacey says, and the feigned fear on her face is replaced with genuine concern.

I take another step backward and trip and fall. The dusty wood of the stage comes up to meet me. I hear a thump and then the sound of clicking heels on wood, and Lacey is beside me.

"Damon. Damon, are you okay?"

"I'm all right," I say. "I just—I don't feel so well."

Mrs. McAvoy's face appears above me, eyebrows drawn together in worry. "Damon, can you hear me?"

"I can hear you just fine," I say.

Jesus, it's not like I fainted, and I'm definitely not deaf.

"Maybe we should call it a day," she says. "You haven't been getting enough rest."

"Okay," I say.

I like how she's decided on an explanation. I'm just tired. Sleep, and all of it will go away, take care of itself.

"We'll pick this up tomorrow," Mrs. McAvoy says. "I'm sure you all could use a break, yes?"

The rest of the cast disperses, but Mrs. McAvoy stays with me. She even sits down on the stage, her long, ruffly skirt spread out beneath her.

"Damon," she says, "I want you to know how much I appreciate the work you're doing on this play."

I blink at her. I still feel dizzy and off balance, even with the solid wood of the stage beneath me.

"Thank you?" I say.

"You're welcome," she says. "I think you're incredibly talented, and that's why I cast you. But I also recognize this is a tough play to do, emotionally. It's a lot for someone to take on who's just transferred to a new school—"

"I can do it," I say. "I know I messed up today, but that doesn't mean—"

"Damon," she says, her voice soft. "I know you can do it.

But if you need to take a break at any time, you can ask for it. Okay?"

The look on her face is one I'm not sure how to read, but I think it's one of understanding.

What do you know? I think, sudden and paranoid, and then push that thought away.

"Okay," I say.

Tristan appears then, a knight in skinny jeans, his eyes wide. He's not in these scenes, though Cassio is certainly a constant presence in Othello's mind at this point in the play. Tristan holds out his hand and helps Mrs. McAvoy to her feet. I get up on my own, slowly and carefully. When I'm standing Tristan places one hand between my shoulder blades and keeps it there, saying, "C'mon, let's go somewhere."

Tristan helps me gather up my stuff, and we both slip on our coats—Tristan's a soft navy peacoat, mine black and puffy and stuffed with down. Tristan leads me along with a press of his fingers to my wrist, out of the school and down the street, and soon we're sitting in a coffee shop a couple blocks away.

I settle into a chair at a fake-wood-covered table. Tristan orders coffee and brings me a cup.

"You didn't have to—" I say, but Tristan waves me off, pushing it across the table. I sip it, savoring the bitter taste. I never sweeten my coffee. I like how coffee tastes when it's being honest.

"So we don't have to talk about it—we can talk about whatever you want."

I stare into my coffee. "I don't know. It's a hard part, I guess."

I can feel Tristan watching me. I know Tristan's not buying what I'm selling, but I don't have enough energy to make this performance convincing.

"We can talk about me instead," Tristan says, taking a sip of his coffee. His drink is topped with a generous helping of whipped cream and probably sweetened into oblivion. "I'm always happy to talk about me."

"Okay," I say.

"So my parents found out I'm gay," Tristan says. "And also, Bryan broke up with me."

My hands twitch around my cardboard cup.

Right. Because I'm not the only person on earth with problems.

"Damn, Tristan. I'm sorry."

"It's been an awesome couple weeks," Tristan says. "I know it has because rehearsing a tragedy that ends in a murder-suicide feels like a relief."

"How did they—"

"We were sloppy," Tristan interrupts. "And to answer your next question, Bryan is a cowardly little shit who couldn't handle the possibility of being outed to his soccer buddies. So here we are. Well—" Tristan shrugs. "Here I am."

"Have you talked to Melanie about it?" I ask. "I mean— I'm guessing you have, but—"

"Not about the breaking up with Bryan part," Tristan says.

His eyes are downcast. Normally Tristan seems unafraid to look the world in the eye.

"I just—I don't know how to talk to her about that. She already thinks I have terrible taste in guys, and I didn't want to—"

"Prove her right?" I say.

"I keep hoping that—this is so stupid, but I keep hoping that maybe he'll want me back," Tristan rushes on. "So pathetic, but I liked him, and . . ."

Tristan trails off, shoulder slumping, and I reach across the table and place my hand on top of Tristan's. I leave my hand there for a moment, then lift it away.

Secrets that hurt you, I want to tell Tristan, *are never worth keeping.*

But I stay silent. Who am I to tell someone that?

"I'm a tool," Tristan says. "I came here to help cheer you up, and all I can do is talk about the most depressing shit in the world."

"Hey, it's not a murder-suicide," I murmur. "That's something."

Tristan looks up, his eyes catching on mine. He looks tired, but there's a victorious glint there too. "Yeah," he says softly. "That's something."

Tristan leaves to go to dinner, but I don't go home. Instead I walk to the Metro and get on and ride to Union Station with all the commuters in suits and shiny shoes. I get off, climb the escalator to Mass. Avenue and start walking in the direction of the Capitol.

One sign proclaims: *Columbus Circle.* Is that what it's

called? I didn't even know that. D.C. has so many circles—fitting, somehow, for a city with few straight lines and fewer straight shooters. There's no city with more secrets than this one, and no secrets less important than mine.

I am not stupid. I know why it's so hard for me to do Othello's final scenes—not because I've ever felt that low or wanted to die, but because the act is real to me in ways it's abstract to others who've only seen it portrayed on TV or in movies or analyzed at an acceptable distance in psych textbooks.

The night Carlos killed himself I sat in the hospital corridor and heard nothing, felt nothing, thought nothing. I clasped my hands together in my lap, absentmindedly trying to do the secret handshake me and Carlos had created one afternoon while feeling bored and aimless. I couldn't do it, couldn't make my hands do the motions required. I remembered the way our fingers interlocked, then the way we tapped fists, but I couldn't remember beyond that—the six or seven other motions. To this day I can't remember how to do it, and it remains one of the many tiny, unimportant things that died with Carlos.

Were there signs? I imagine there were, but I wasn't looking for them. How do you look for what you don't know is there? Sure, Carlos was moody, angry, and unpredictable. He got me to do crazy things, things I'd never do on my own: steal, tag trains with brightly colored aerosol spray paint, hit on girls ten years older and out of my league. Carlos's family was fucked up, no doubt:

His mother was an emotional basket case and his dad was hardly ever around, and when he was he never did anything but scream and throw punches. Carlos worked all the time at his cousin's auto repair shop, bought groceries, played the part of man of the house, took care of his baby sisters.

But that's not the whole story, and I know it. Carlos loved his family. If he'd seen any other way, he never would have left them behind.

Not unless he thought there was some reason they wouldn't want him around.

Why couldn't you just tell me?

But I know why he couldn't tell me. Because he was afraid of what I would think. Of what it would mean for us, for our friendship. Because all this time that I thought Carlos was telling me everything, he was keeping the one thing from me that mattered most.

I scuff my shoe against the frosted ground. My head aches.

Afterward everyone reassured me, over and over again, that it wasn't my fault. I just bit my lip and nodded, but I wanted to tell them: *It is my fault. It is my fault. It is my fault.*

The shrink I went to only once asked me: *Where do you feel it? Where do you feel your grief?* I said: *Everywhere. Everywhere.* I meant in my body—my chest, my head, my stomach, the tips of my fingers and the ends of my toes—but also everywhere outside of me, on every corner, in every store, under the covers, on that boat we used for crew, everywhere, everywhere, everywhere. Everywhere I point the camera, in every image I capture, in everything I see and don't see because Carlos isn't there to fill the space.

Damon, my father said to me with heavy-lidded eyes the morning after, *it's okay if you want to talk—*

No, I said, and shut myself up in my room for the rest of the day. I spent those lonely hours learning the ways of Carlos's camera, reading the manual I found online, taking photos of my shoes, my unmade bed, the view out my window, making sure each one was perfectly in focus, had even contrast and color saturation and tone.

This was one thing I could do, I thought. I could make people see this world the way it is: how beautiful, how amazing and how fucked up.

Sometimes I tug out the box of photos from under my bed and flip through them just so I can see Carlos—see his face and remember. *I'm so sorry,* I want to say. *I'm so sorry I didn't see you, that I didn't get it, that I didn't know until it was too late. I'm so sorry I was too late. People keep saying they're sorry, but fuck that, fuck them—I'm sorry, I'm the one who's sorry, I wish I could tell you that, I wish there was some way you could know how sorry I am.*

For in my sense 'tis happiness to die. Every time I come to that line I trip over it, a pebble in my path. How could Carlos have thought that? How could he have thought it would be better or easier? How could he have thought these things when I was here and his friend?

Even if the world had nothing else to offer Carlos, it still had me.

I am still here.

But I couldn't be what Carlos wanted, not really. Carlos knew that. Carlos knew it even if I didn't.

Othello continues:

> *When you shall these unlucky deeds relate,*
> *Speak of me as I am. Nothing extenuate,*
> *Nor set down aught in malice.*

Speak of me as I am. I don't know how to do that for Carlos, not yet, but I want to be able to do it. I don't only want to have Carlos's camera, I want to be that camera. I want to frame Carlos's world, to freeze it in time. I want people to know who Carlos was, to see what he saw, to feel what he felt, to know. I want people to know.

I sit down on the steps of the Library of Congress, wrapping my hands around my knees and rocking back and forth. It's cold now; night has fallen and my cheeks are wet. I'll pretend it's because of the cold. There are few people around—the young, underpaid staffers are shut up in their offices, tourists have gone out to dinner or back to their hotels, and it feels like a ghost town.

I pull out the camera and snap a tilted picture of the Capitol, lit from below the dome, glowing like a beacon. The Capitol was supposed to be the highest point in D.C., built on a hill so everyone could see it. Not many people know that. If this city were a tree, the Capitol would be the seed from which it sprouted and spread.

I get back on the Metro and ride to Woodley Park, then get off at the zoo and walk, just follow my feet where they want to go. I find the spot in the park more easily this time. Every time it gets a little easier. Like rubbing a bruise: hurts more as it fades away.

In my mind, I see Carlos waiting beneath the tree when I get there, propped up against it. He could be lounging. I remember thinking: *He could be resting, he could just be resting.*

The fury hits me like a thunderbolt, sudden and irrational and unexpected. I can see Carlos there, and he's so smug, and he's so confusing, and God. God.

I hate you, I think. *I hate you, Carlos.*

You don't mean that.

I mean it, I think, and viciously kick over a pile of leaves. *I think you're a selfish bastard.*

I see you've entered the next stage of grief, Carlos says. *Anger.*

"Oh, fuck you, man," I say, and start at the sound of my own voice, so loud in the quiet.

I didn't do it, I think. *I didn't kill you, I didn't—*

Yeah, but you let me die.

I curl my hands into fists. The anger is so potent now, swirling dark inside of me, whispering fierce.

Fuck you, man, I think. *You put all of this on me. You decided, you made that decision, and you lied—you lied to me. You told me you were okay. We made plans that night to hang out, a couple DVDs and some KFC, but you made plans too and you didn't tell me about them. You never did that before, man, you never—you never lied. I thought you never—but that wasn't true either, was it? You lied every time you told me you were okay, every time you acted like—*

You're the actor, D. You telling me you couldn't read the signs? The letters on the wall?

Men should be what they seem, I think, Iago's words echoing in my ears. *I'm the actor, but you're the photographer. The camera never lies. Right?*

The camera lies all the time, hombre. I don't mean airbrushing and all that shit—I mean when you hold that thing in your hand and focus, you're showing people what you see, right? But you're also deciding what you don't want them to see. Whatever's outside the frame. People always talk about what the camera exposes. They never talk about what it hides.

I exhale, a deep, full breath. The wind ruffles the leaves in the trees and it's like they're exhaling with me, one big release. But I'm no more relaxed, and Carlos is gone.

He's gone.

The next day at school, I round a corner and nearly run face-first into Prague. He grabs my arm.

Yesterday when I talked to Prague, I walked out on him. Now he's looking kind of sheepish—not an expression I'm used to seeing on his smug-ass face.

"Can we talk?" Prague asks.

"Depends on what you want to talk about," I say.

I don't mean to be unkind, but I'm tired of the lectures and condescension—don't do the play, it's too gay; don't date the white girl, you'll piss people off. I'm tired of coloring within the lines. I played it so safe with Carlos, never pushed him to talk, never asked the questions that nudged at the back of my mind: *How bad is it? How scared are you? Do you know you're not alone?*

"I wanted to talk about Melanie," Prague says.

"I don't know if I want to talk to you about her," I say.

"That's fair," Prague says. "But I'm sorry, man."

It's a genuine apology, sudden and unqualified. I don't know what to say.

"You trying to say it's suddenly okay for me to date a white girl?" I ask.

Prague sighs. "I'm saying you should date who you want. And I—"

He stops for a second, scratching behind his ear.

"My boy Trey said Melanie's mom was his little sister's art teacher. He said she died this last summer, cancer or some shit. Nobody even knew she was sick. And I thought—"

That I might understand what that's like, I finish for him. I draw in a breath.

"I'm not trying to mess shit up for you, D," Prague says. "Maybe you think that, but . . . I just want you to be okay."

I look at him, and our eyes meet.

"Yeah," I say. "Well."

"You do what you need to do, is what I'm saying," Prague says. "Whatever gets you through the day."

I don't even know what to say to that. Who is this Prague and what's he done with my dumbass cousin?

"And plus, she looks like she could kick your ass," Prague says, quickly. "So maybe that's what you need."

I stare at Prague for a long moment, long enough for Prague to start to look queasy.

Then I begin to laugh, and soon Prague is laughing too.

On Friday I show up promptly at seven at Melanie's house for our date, dressed in a pair of gray slacks and a long-sleeve button-down shirt with a leather jacket over it. Melanie's wearing a long black skirt and a gauzy black top, silver eyeliner making her eyes sparkle.

"You look amazing," I say, and lean forward and press a kiss to her cheek. I rest my hand on her arm, and she leans in.

I wonder when she started doing that—when she started leaning in.

"Thanks," she says. "You look pretty good yourself."

"I know I do," I say. "I worked hard on the hair today. Used a comb and everything. You ready for a ride in my sexy car?"

"You mean your Volvo?"

"It's my parents' Volvo, okay, and that Volvo is hot," I say. "There is no Volvo hotter than that Volvo."

"I think your Volvo might be the anti-sexy," she says.

"That's kind of mean, Ellis. I'm offended, and more importantly, my Volvo's offended. As my mother would say, it's a sensible vehicle. Not much good being sexy if you're dead."

Melanie cocks her head to one side. "That's a good point."

"So get in my anti-sexy Volvo," I say, opening the door for her, "and let's blow this joint."

When we're both situated I flick on the ignition and the car rumbles to life, the stereo filling the car with the dry, sardonic drawl of Etta James.

"I think we can agree," I say, "that having me in this Volvo makes it sexier."

Melanie turns to me and grins.

"Well, of course, sugar."

"Now I'm gonna take you somewhere," I say.

"Surprise me, Casanova," she says, and smiles.

"Somewhere" is Five Guys for burgers, and then a building near Fannie Mae in Tenleytown. The building is a standard office building, but when we go around the side I go straight for the door I know will be unlocked and push it open. Thanks to Carlos, I know at least a half dozen office buildings that don't lock their doors and don't have working alarms. I lead Melanie into the darkened hallway and jam my finger into the button to call the elevator. When it arrives, we climb inside. The elevator has dirty lime green carpet and faux wood walls.

"This is officially the strangest place I have ever been at nine o'clock on a Friday night," Melanie tells me. "I really hope you're not a serial killer."

"Whatever, I got you burgers," I say with a wave of my hand. "What are you complaining about? This is totally romantic."

Truthfully, I would have been happy to buy Melanie pricier food, but I'd been excited to bring her here. I think she'll like what she sees.

"How do you know about this place?" Melanie asks.

"A friend told me about it. It's quiet. And private."

"Unless we get caught."

I shrug. I'm not worried. *You get caught, you tell 'em you're part of the cleaning crew,* Carlos said once. *Nobody ever suspects a black or Latino kid with a mop.*

The elevator door dings and opens on a long, narrow corridor. I lead her up a staircase, then shove open an ugly green door. A cool fall breeze greets us, ruffling Melanie's hair. She's warm beside me and she smells delicious, like french fry salt and spice.

We step out on the rooftop and walk to the edge. The building's not tall—no buildings in D.C. are higher than fifteen stories, as mandated by law, nothing higher than the Capitol—but it has a nice view of downtown in one direction and the low rooftops of town houses in the other. The sky rolls out in front of us, empty and huge and lovely. Being up here makes the air look solid, like we could step out onto that darkness and feel it beneath our feet, firm as asphalt.

"Wow," Melanie whispers.

"Yeah."

I look at her, scarlet-tinted hair bright under the security lights, dark eyes glittering, lips bitten to the red of her hair.

I lean in.

I kiss her, and oh, I've kissed her before, but this feels

different. My tongue flicks at her bottom lip, asking for permission like I'm knocking on her front door. She opens her mouth against mine and suddenly it's another level of kissing, slippery and deep and dirty and *wow*.

I pull the clip out of her hair, run my hand through the strands and tip her head back so I can kiss her some more. I feel the warmth collecting in my stomach, fuzzy and hot. She tastes vaguely like a burger and ketchup, and she makes this sweet little strangled sound when I press my hand to her cheek.

When we separate to breathe she murmurs, "You got me up here so we could make out? Is that what you're trying to tell me?"

I stroke the back of her neck with one hand, a smirk playing at the corners of my mouth.

"Well, yeah."

She pinches me in retaliation, and I pinch her back, and her grin spreads from one side of her face to the other like a sunrise.

"Live a little, Melanie Ellis," I breathe against her lips, and then I'm kissing her again.

This time I push so she's up against the wall. Melanie makes an irritated noise when her hair gets tangled behind her, but she's not stopping me. I can feel the rush everywhere, the flush everywhere, the slow-rolling heat.

"Does that line work with all the girls?" Melanie mumbles against my lips, and I trace a finger over the exposed skin of her hip where her shirt's ridden up.

"Not really," I say. "Just you."

She gives me a shove, but her hands stay grasping my shirt, like she wants to pull me closer, not push me away.

This close I can see the places where her eyelashes stick together with mascara, the smooth line of her eyeliner, the tiny scar at the corner of her left eye.

"Where did you get that?" I ask, brushing over the scar with my thumb.

"When I was six," she says. "Tripped and fell, got scratched up by a branch. The doctor said I was lucky not to lose my eye."

"That would've sucked," I say, and I know I sound like an idiot, but my brain is overwhelmed with the feeling of her body so near mine.

"It definitely would've," Melanie says.

I lean down to press a kiss to her lips.

"I like it," I murmur.

"You're demented," she whispers back.

Melanie

It happens at least twenty times a day. I do something or say something or see something and I want to send a postcard to that place where you are with no address: WISH YOU WERE HERE.

CHAPTER EIGHT

I wake up with a tingling hum under my skin. I dreamed about Damon, his hands everywhere: along the inside of my thighs, at the small of my back, fingers tracing over the knobby bones of my knees, pressing into my belly button, flickering over my collarbone, thumbs tilting my chin, angling my face.

This happened. This happened to me.

Well, maybe it didn't happen exactly like that. Maybe it happened on a windy rooftop, and mostly we kissed, and it was less like a romance novel and more like a wrestling match, with too many limbs involved and not enough dexterity. And yet I never felt claustrophobic or scared, never wanted to be anywhere else. The only thing we needed was space for our bodies to move, and all we wanted to do was share that space between us.

I yawn and stretch, flip over my cell phone to see the time, and notice I have new messages. Who is texting me at the crack of dawn on Saturday? I swipe it open and check—Tristan, of course. Six messages, composing a poem of increasing desperation.

    can we talk?
    i'm not doing so great.
    i need to talk.
    meet me for lunch.

or before. meet me before.

meet me now?

I blink, then rub at my eyes. The last message is time-stamped 6:26 a.m., only a few minutes ago.

I dial his number and am not surprised when he picks it up on the first ring.

"Hey," Tristan says. His voice sounds scratchy.

"Tell me where," I say. "I'll be there."

We meet on Wisconsin near the Metro, walk down past Best Buy and duck into Morty's. Tristan orders coffee and a bagel and I get french toast, figuring that whatever's going on with him, it might require the energy provided by a full stomach. We sit in a corner booth. Tristan shreds his napkin into tiny pieces, then scatters them across the table like snow.

"Tell me about Damon," he says.

I blink. "What about Damon, exactly?"

"How are things going with you two?" Tristan asks. "You had another date, right?"

A date, right. Fast food and fast kisses.

"Things are going really well."

Tristan scratches the back of his neck. He's all quick movements today, twitches and shivers. I want to reach out and hold him still, to say: *Breathe.*

"That's good," Tristan says. "That's awesome, that's amazing. I'm so happy for you."

He doesn't sound happy for me. He doesn't sound happy.

"Tristan, what's up?" I say. "You leave me this string of texts on a Saturday morning, and—"

"My parents want me to go see a therapist," Tristan interrupts. "They said it was because they were worried about me, but I know it's because they want someone to, like, talk me out of being gay. The therapist is one of my dad's friends. I said no, and they said if I didn't go I couldn't be in the play. So I guess I'm going to a therapist."

"Oh, God," I say. "This is how your dad thinks he can cure you?"

"Apparently," Tristan says.

"Maybe he's scared," I murmur.

"Of course he's fucking scared," Tristan says. "Probably the first time in my life my dad's ever been scared of me."

I glance up to meet Tristan's eyes, and God, he looks furious. I don't think I've ever seen Tristan look that angry before.

Yes, Tristan. Yes.

"Maybe he should be scared," I say.

His blue eyes flicker almost green, but then they dim dark. The table is covered with pieces of napkin now, victims of Tristan's anxious fingers.

"Speaking of scared," Tristan says. "Bryan kind of . . . ended our thing."

I suck in a breath. I knew it. Fucking closet case, I knew he'd be a bastard. But there is no comfort in this thought, in being right.

"If he doesn't see what he's got in you—"

"I know, he's an asshole who doesn't deserve me, et cetera, et cetera," Tristan cuts me off. "I get it, I don't need the lecture."

"Tristan—"

"I see the way you look at me," Tristan says, biting off each word. "Like, oh, Tristan, he's so adorable, he's got a crush."

"I never said that," I say. "You're putting words in my mouth."

"I know you think I'm an idiot for dating him," Tristan says. "You think he's just some dumb jock, that all the guys I want to date don't have two brain cells to rub together. He's not like that, though. He's—"

"Jesus," I say, temper flaring. "You want me to be a part of this conversation, or you doing okay without me?"

Tristan sighs. He scratches one fingernail over the surface of the tabletop, Formica squeaking.

"French toast?"

The waitress places a large plate of breakfast in front of me, but suddenly I'm not hungry. I push my plate away.

Look at me, please, just—

But Tristan keeps his eyes on the table, fingers curling into a fist.

On Monday I don't really want to go to rehearsal, but I have to. Opening night of the play is drawing nearer and Calvin's starting to freak out in his own unique, subtly detectable way. Last time I showed up ten minutes late, he stared at me for a full fifteen seconds without blinking, then narrowed his eyes to indicate his displeasure. It was very disconcerting.

Tristan's not going to be at rehearsal today—they aren't

running his scenes. I'm relieved, because I don't know what to say to him right now. Tristan has a right to be angry, and anything I say sounds like a lame attempt at smothering that furious flame. Tristan's got enough people telling him what he feels is wrong. I don't want to be one of them, another hollow, insistent voice in the crowd.

In the auditorium Damon spots me and bounds across the aisle to tug me into an embrace. He kisses me on the mouth, paying no attention to the whoops and cheers that erupt around us from the gathering cast, and lifts his hand to give them all the finger. He winds one hand through my hair, twisting. His lips are warm against mine.

When we break apart I say, breathless, "What was that for?"

"Time to rehearse, my darlings!" Mrs. McAvoy shouts, and everyone begins to disperse.

Damon grins at me and takes off for the stage.

I've got no choice but to go backstage and pretend like I didn't just get a little weak in the knees. Calvin hands me a brush, pursing his lips. Max clomps past me in combat boots making kissy noises. I studiously ignore them.

The scenery is starting to look like something real now—it's sort of amazing. The castle walls appear 3-D, and the arched supports look as if they might actually be able to bear weight. Much of this is Calvin's work, his precision and care and experience, but I like being a part of it too. So what if most of what I do is fill in between the lines as if the whole set was some giant paint-by-numbers? When Calvin stops by and gives me an approving nod, I feel warm and accomplished.

On my break, I take my usual spot in the wings. They're rehearsing tough stuff today: the final act. I watch the scene unfold. Karen as Emilia, Desdemona's handmaiden, discovers Desdemona sprawled on the bed. Damon stands stiff and frozen in a corner, paralyzed with what he's just done.

"O falsely, falsely murdered," Lacey murmurs from the bed. Her hair is a mass of tangled curls, white dress fanned out around her, lacy and delicate.

"O Lord, what cry is that?" Karen looks around, wild-eyed.

"That? What?"

"Out, and alas, that was my lady's voice!" Karen shrieks, stumbling over to the bed. "Help! Help ho! Help! O lady, speak again! Sweet Desdemona, O sweet mistress, speak!"

Karen shakes Lacey's supine body. Lacey lifts her head from the pillow and gasps out, "A guiltless death I die."

Karen shouts, "O, who hath done this deed?"

"Nobody," Lacey whispers. "I myself."

Damon makes a sound in the back of his throat, reaches out for the wall and grasps at air.

"Farewell. Commend me to my kind lord," Lacey moans. "O, farewell."

"Why, how should she be murdered?" Damon asks. His voice is thin and nasal, as if he's not getting enough oxygen.

"Good, Damon," Mrs. McAvoy calls from her seat in the audience.

"Alas, who knows?" Karen asks.

"You heard her say herself, it was—it was not I," Damon stutters.

"She said so," Karen affirms. "I must needs report the truth."

Damon's hands are shaking. He's breathing as if he's just run a seven-minute mile.

I move forward. Is he—

"She's like a liar gone to burning hell!" Damon grits out. "'Twas I that killed . . . 'twas I—"

But Damon can't say it. He stands completely still for a moment, an unmoving tree, then turns and walks toward the wings. His eyes are locked on me, but it's like he's not seeing me at all. He brushes past me without a word.

I can hear the mumble tumble of raised voices onstage, the murmured confusion, Mrs. McAvoy saying, "Damon, do you need to see the nurse?"

All I can see is Damon.

"Hey," I say, breathless, and reach out. I touch skin, wrap my hand around his arm and hold on. "Damon—"

"Please leave me alone."

"I don't want to," I say.

"Melanie," Damon says, and my name sounds wrong, like a song sung out of tune.

"Talk to me," I say. "What happened?"

"I fucked up," Damon mutters.

"It's just a play, you know. Can't you—"

"It's not—" Damon backs away so fast, I think I might have left scratch marks.

"It's not what?" I ask. "Not easy? I realize that. But—"

"It's not the fucking play," he says.

His eyes are the silver-green of snake scales, sharp and bright.

Why is he angry at me? He practically mauls me before rehearsal, and now he won't even talk to me?

I am so tired of talking in uncertainties and vague hints, of trying to decode the words of the people I love—Tristan, Damon, my dad. My mom, who didn't want me to know until it was too late. I'm so sick of this dance. Dancing with someone is only fun if that person understands your movements and wants to make them with you, not trip you up and watch you stumble.

"I want to help you," I say slowly. "But I can't help you if you don't talk to me. Why are you upset with me? Everything seemed so—"

"You can't help me," Damon says.

His voice is low, controlled. It chills me to my marrow.

"Hey," I hear, and Lacey is there. "Damon, are you—"

"I'm fine," Damon says.

"You're not fine," I say. "You're not—"

"Don't tell me what I feel," Damon says, sharp.

Lacey backs away. I hear her talking to other cast members. She's probably telling them we're having some kind of romantic tiff. Lacey loves gossip.

"Maybe I can help you," I say. "How do you know whether I can help you if you don't tell—"

"You don't understand," Damon says, whipping back around. "And I can't make you understand."

"I understand Othello fine, and he's plenty fucked up," I snap. "Why couldn't I understand what's going on with you?"

Damon's face falls. "I don't mean—"

"What the hell do you mean, then?" I ask.

Damon won't look at me. He won't look at me and he won't talk to me and he won't let me touch him, and why should I be patient with someone who pushes me away?

"You said this was a play about grief," Damon says. "About losing, right?"

I'm so angry.

"Maybe it's a play about some asshole who strangles his wife," I bite back. "Maybe he's a douchebag who made his own bed. He didn't really *lose* her, did he? He didn't misplace her. It's like you just said. *'Twas I who*—"

"Jesus Christ, Melanie," Damon hisses. "I know the lines. I know the play. I mean that it's more complicated than that—losing someone."

"I know that," I say. "I know a little bit about grief too."

"I know you do," Damon says. "I'm not trying to say—"

"What are you trying to say, then?" I say.

It's Damon who reaches out this time, but I pull away. I can feel the fabric of my shirt rub against my skin as I press back into the wall.

"I'm sorry," he says.

All these sorrys, these apologies for what's wrong with the world, all the regrets and sympathies and condolences in the universe.

None of them will ever bring my mother back.

Maybe I can't understand him. Maybe he's right. And he can't understand me.

Nobody can understand.

"Just stop," I say. "Don't tell me you're sorry."

I step away, feeling the air fill the space between our bodies. I can see him standing there, shoulders rising and falling, body contorted with breath.

"I can't do this," I blurt out.

"I—"

I turn and run, and run, and run, run out of the theater and the school and over many blocks, around cars and past houses. The sound bleeds and blurs around me, a noisy smudge.

By the time I reach my front porch I'm heaving, arms wrapped around my middle. I lean against my front door for a moment, feeling the wood press into my skin.

I hate crying—the way it feels, the tears messing up my eye makeup and staining my cheeks red and making my eyes puffy and bloodshot. I hate breathing like this: the panting, choked-off sighs, the tightness in my chest.

I unlock the front door and climb the steps to my bedroom. It's a mess. My room never used to be a mess. Mom was always vigilant about it: *Melly, keep it clean. A messy room is a messy mind.*

Well, yeah. My mind is a mess. *I am a mess without you, Mom. I am a total disaster.*

I want to kick something. I want it to hurt. I want to throw things like she did. I want to be angry. I'm so fucking *angry.*

I kick the bed frame. It rattles and shakes. I kick it harder and the whole bed moves, but it's not enough. I want—

I see the corner of something under the bed, cardboard edged with red.

I know what it is. It's my sketchbook.

There's a part of me that wants to shove it under the bed and forget it exists, but I'm drawn to it. I lean down and pick it up and flip it open.

The drawings seem infantile. Derivative, because that's what they are. Copies of things. I page through them—a feral Wolverine, Mickey Mouse. People I saw in the park. A vague sketch of Tristan. Silly stuff, kid stuff.

This is all I do, even after all this time. Imitate. Make boring art. Fade into the background.

Except. Except then I flip the page, and there are these. The drawings of my mom I did when she was sick. God. I forgot about these. It's a grim sort of flipbook, each one showing her a little thinner, a little less like my mom.

Turning the pages is like watching her die all over again.

In the last one she is asleep, the contours of her face smooth, narrow, peaceful. I touch my finger to the page but it's just paper. It's not skin. It's not her.

It's not her.

I turn the page to see what comes next.

I didn't do this.

Two whole pages are covered in my mom's handwriting. It's shaky, so I know it's recent, from her last weeks when her hands weren't steady anymore.

Dearest Melly,

I don't know how long it will take you to find this. I hope it's not too long. I hope you're not angry that I found this and looked through it. Whenever I find art it's hard for me to put it away without looking. So I looked.

I think you would say this isn't art. That's what you always claimed—that you weren't an artist, not like me. You're free to be what you wish and do what you want but I hope you know how beautiful this is, Melly. How beautiful you are and how talented. You are so talented and so beautiful. I wish I had told you that more.

We are very different, you and I. Maybe it's been hard for you sometimes, having a mother like me. Dad tells me I can be kind of a lot and I know he's right.

The thing is, I wasn't always like this. I used to be more scared and quiet and sad. Maybe it's hard for you to believe that, but it's true. I spent two years in college pretending I was going to major in business because my parents wanted me to do something practical. Those years weren't wasted because later I would use that knowledge to help your father open a restaurant! But they were sad years. They were lonely. And so I made a different choice.

It wasn't that simple. It never is. But I know you can do it. You're brave.

The thing about knowing you're dying is that it puts everything in perspective. It makes you think: What matters to me? What do I care about? When I found out about the cancer I knew I needed to make art and be with you and your father. That was what mattered to me. It still is. I'm so grateful for this life. I'm so grateful for you, Melly.

I don't think you need my advice because you are already so wise, but I will leave you with this: Don't hide the things that matter. Let yourself be seen. Let people know you. However you do it is up to you. But just don't hide. It's so lonely, and the world is so big and beautiful. Let yourself explore and be as big and beautiful as this world.

I know you will be okay after I'm gone because you're strong, but please, please know that you're not alone.

You are not alone.

I will say it again: You are not alone.

And as long as you remember me, I will be here. I love you, sweetheart.

She signed it big and dramatic like always, all flourishes and twists: *DANA.*

The first thing I think is: *What am I supposed to do with this?*

I put the sketchbook back down on the bed and close it. My hands are shaking.

I go down into the basement because I know it'll be dark and quiet. I nearly stumble down the stairs before I remember I should probably turn on the light. I want privacy, not a concussion. The light flickers on, illuminating my mother's reconstructed studio. There's paint everywhere, drying in open containers, flaking off the sides of cans and gunked on brushes, color streaking every surface because Mom wouldn't have it any other way. It looks like she could come back at any minute, show up and pick up a brush and make something beautiful.

I run my hand over the surface of one of the tables. The pad of my finger catches on a splinter of wood. I wince, bringing my hand to my mouth and sucking away the tiny dot of blood. It tastes bitter and salty, like sweat.

I flip through her open sketchbook spread out on the table. It's filled with figure drawings: a few of neighborhood children, some of Dad, some nudes Mom probably did at the community college when they had models. I turn the page and there's my own face staring back at me from a series of colored pencil drawings. I've never seen them before. My hair is a smudged red while the rest of my face is etched in black and white. It looks like my hair is on fire. In one sketch my hair curls upward as if windblown, tendrils flying everywhere, a messy burning halo. Mom must have done it within the last few months. My hair hasn't been red for very long.

I used to be the girl who blended in with the cinderblock walls, who people sort of liked but who didn't really register, who got along and put up and shut up. Now I'm a tattoo—scarred, scary. I'm a fluttering touch that's become a brand.

But even in the costume I've created, stitched together from patches of my sanity, I'm still working backstage, still trying to blend into the scenery I help create. I've never wanted to be in the spotlight, never considered what it would be like to be watched with such intensity and focus. My mother got up in front of a class and taught. She put on art shows and left it all out there for people to see. I lurk in the shadows.

Let yourself be seen.

Today Damon was the one up on that stage, being watched, playing the part of the horror-stricken fallen warrior. All that talk of losing and grief, and somehow I forgot—forgot what it means that Damon has lost someone too.

Was. You said he was.

Carlos and his camera, Carlos who got Damon in trouble. Carlos with the winning smile in that photo Damon gave me. Carlos who would have liked me.

Your words and performances are no kin together, Roderigo rails at the crafty Iago. But I'm beginning to wonder if

Damon's are too much kin, if Othello's grief is melting into his own.

We all act out our parts so people don't see the tricky, knotted-up mess inside of us, but sometimes we don't do such a flawless job, and the messy part peeks out between our frightened fingers.

He'd said: *You don't understand.*

What don't I understand? What don't I see?

I trace one finger down over the page, following the vapor trails left by my mother's pencil. The paper feels smooth under the pads of my fingers. My tears are coming faster now, coming and coming and coming. I lift a brush from one of the glass jars Mom used to house them and unscrew the top from a jar of red paint. Both brush and paint are not quite wet enough, but they're sufficiently liquid for me to spread the red over the drawing in broad, swirly shapes.

I paint and cry and cry and paint until my face disappears from the page.

That night I lie there on my soft cotton sheets with my eyes closed, trying to think about nothing, but my mind insists on repeating one line from *Othello* over and over like a mantra:

Man but a rush against Othello's breast,
And he retires. Where should Othello go?

Around 4:00 a.m. I give up on sleep, fumble for my cell phone and turn it on. I turned it off when I left rehearsal, not wanting to talk to anyone, especially Damon. I still don't know what to say to him, not yet.

Sure enough, it beeps to indicate I have a message, and I tap my screen to get into my voice mail with trembling fingers.

It's Tristan. His voice is high and tight with worry.

"Melanie, are you okay? I went to look for you at rehearsal and you were gone and . . . whatever you need, just—just call me. I don't care if it's the middle of the night, call me. Whatever this is, I don't want you to be alone with it."

I don't think; I call him. Tristan picks up on the first ring.

"Talk to me," he says.

It should be easy in the way that it's always been easy for me to talk to Tristan, ever since we were little and used to sit around building castles out of Legos and discussing the houses we wanted to own someday. Tristan wanted a house made of windows. I still remember that, now, because it was so quintessentially, perfectly Tristan. He never thought he had anything to hide.

"Tell me about Bryan," I say. "Tell me what happened."

There's a startled intake of breath, then rustling. I imagine Tristan shifting in bed, getting comfortable, nestling under the covers.

"I don't know what you want me to tell you, Mel."

"Anything," I say. "Tell me anything."

He sighs. The phone fuzzes over with static.

"He's scared," Tristan says. "I'm scared too, but I'm not as scared as he is."

I gaze out the window at the impenetrable dark. The sun will rise soon, peel these shadows off like old skin.

"You can't be with someone who's more scared than you are," Tristan says. "I think that's what I've figured out. You can be scared together, but only in equal amounts."

God, that's it. We're both so scared, but we don't know how to be scared together.

"Damon and I had a fight," I blurt out. "I don't even know what it was about, but it was . . . bad."

"Bad how?" Tristan asks.

"I don't know," I say. "I think I said some stuff that I shouldn't have."

"He's been having a lot of trouble at rehearsal," Tristan says. "He freaked out last week, you know. Basically collapsed in the middle of a scene onstage."

"I didn't know that," I say. "Today too—he couldn't finish a scene."

"Oh man, really?" Tristan says. "That's awful."

"Damon's not really—open with me," I say. "I mean, sometimes he is. But sometimes he isn't."

"Yeah, well, I hate to tell you this, Melly," Tristan says, "but you're not exactly an open book yourself."

I stay silent.

"He probably doesn't want you to worry about him," Tristan says. "He seems like the kind of guy that doesn't like to cause a lot of trouble for people."

He tried to tell me this time. He wanted me to know—

I think of Damon sliding the photograph across the table in the diner.

Sometimes it feels like he's . . . watching. Like he knows what's going on and wants to be a part of it. You know?

I think: *Push me, push me,* but that's so unfair, so wrong, to want Tristan to extract this information from me. It's not his job to do that.

"You can talk to me, you know," Tristan says. "Whenever you want, about whatever you want."

The more I think about it, the more I'm sure that Carlos was Damon's Tristan.

How do you even quantify a loss like that?

"Thank you," I say.

"No need to thank me," Tristan says. "Like you said, we're BFFs. It's part of the package."

I find my mouth trying to turn up at the edges, lift into a smile.

"I know you were really into Bryan," I say. "I thought maybe it wasn't serious, that it was just because he's a hot soccer player and stuff, but . . . I saw the way you looked when you were talking about him. I'm sorry, Tristan. About everything."

I deflate, feeling winded. I make a looping gesture with my hand that I realize too late he can't see.

"Man, Melanie. I . . . I'm not even sure what to say." Tristan clears his throat. "I liked Bryan, yeah, but I think I liked him more than he deserved. I liked sneaking around with him. It was sexy, having that secret. But secrets aren't sexy forever, and he would've been happy keeping me a secret. There's a fine line between having a secret and being ashamed."

I wish Tristan was here, right now. I want to press our hands together, a hand sandwich. It's something we've been doing since our middle school did *Romeo & Juliet* and Tristan was Romeo—*for saints have hands that pilgrims' hands do touch, and palm to palm is holy palmers' kiss.* I still love how smooth Tristan's palms are against mine, how his touch makes me feel safe. Tristan will always feel like home, no matter how far I run and where I hide.

"I will miss this thing he did with his tongue, though," Tristan says thoughtfully. "It was, like, this twist—"

"Tristan, I love you," I interrupt him, hiccuping out a laugh.

"I love you too," Tristan says. There's a touch of laughter there, but I know he means it.

"You're amazing," I say.

"I know."

I wake up the next morning, glance at my calendar and realize it's Halloween. Halloween doesn't mean the same things it did to me as a kid—too-sweet candy corn, costumes, pumpkins, monsters jumping out of the darkness, scary— but it feels timely. Halloween is supposed to be about exorcising demons, about bringing the bad to the surface, and Lord knows the demons in my life have come out to play.

That night I meet Tristan at his house at dusk and we

wander around our neighborhood, admiring the jack-o'-lanterns with jagged mouths and slits for eyes, the sticky cobwebs clinging to doorways, the rickety skeletons dangling in windows. Kids tromp by in costumes, toting plastic buckets and bags, giggling and hyper, trailed by parents too tired to attempt discipline.

Tristan and I started doing this four years ago when we declared ourselves too old to trick-or-treat but didn't want to get conned into handing out candy either. We're not quite celebrating the holiday, but we're participating, observing. It's a little creepy, maybe, but it keeps us busy. Tonight we tramp through the leaves, wet from recent rain, and stuff our hands into each other's pockets to keep them warm.

"Do you wish we could trick-or-treat?" Tristan asks, shuffling over the sidewalk in an awkward hybrid dance that resembles a two-step/Lindy-Hop combo, lots of twisty flips of the ankle. "I still think I would have been an awesome Marilyn."

I shrug and push my hair behind my ear. "I used to like it. Dressing up. Campaigning for candy."

"But now you dress up every day, freak show," Tristan teases, nudging me with his shoulder. "I always felt like there was a competitive edge to the whole deal, a viciousness to the candy economy. Very dog-eat-dog. Everybody obsessed with material gain. That's not healthy."

I laugh, but it stings, a little. *You dress up every day, freak show.* Costumes. Playing parts. Secrets. Secrets are one step away from shame. I can't help it: I think of Damon. I think of him on that rooftop, and him on that stage, and how these people are the same person, but not the same at all.

All I want is to be able to *see* him more clearly, to bring him into focus like one of his photographs, like that photograph of Carlos he gave me months ago, because he wanted me to see what he had lost.

I take pictures 'cause it makes you look close, Damon had said.

But Damon is no photograph, no still image frozen in time. Damon is not going to open up like some kind of spring flower if I just wait long enough.

I need to look closer, and I need to show him what I see.

"Hey," I say. "Let's go to school."

"Just for fun?" Tristan says. "That may be the lamest idea you've ever had."

"I have an idea," I say. "I need to look at the scenery for the play."

"The scenery for the—" Tristan stares at me. "Did you forget your meds today?"

"C'mon," I say, and tug Tristan along.

To his credit, Tristan only resists a little. Or a lot, but he gives up eventually, once it's clear that I'm not listening.

"If I get expelled for this, you are the one who's going to explain it to my dad," Tristan says as I pick the old lock on the crumbling back door that leads into the gym.

"We won't get caught," I say.

"You say that," Tristan says, "but you always used to lose at hide-and-seek, so—"

"Then stay here," I say, and take off across the gym.

"I like this plan," Tristan calls out. "It gives me plausible deniability."

"You don't even know what that means," I say.

"Whatever, I watch TV!"

I don't mind—I know this is something I need to do alone anyway. When I round a corner and push open the doors to the theater, my breath catches. It smells musty, as if the ghosts of past productions linger in the air, characters reincarnated, brought to life, then abandoned like old clothes to collect mothballs and memories.

I'm backstage in seconds, standing in front of the scenery. Cyprus looms before me: the inside of the castle, a lot of gray and black and square angles. Outside the castle there's nothing—just a lot of empty, undefined space.

I had been so eager to tell Damon what the play means. I should have told him this instead: *You are not Othello. You are not him, because Othello has nowhere to go.*

Damon does. I need to show him where.

I examine the backdrop, let my eyes skim over the images until they cohere into a full picture in my mind. Then I pick up a brush, dip it in green, lift it to the border, and begin to paint.

DAMON

Dude, no. No way.
Why not?
Because she's ugly.
That's fucked up.
I'm not saying I—
You think there might be girls talking shit about you, like,
    Oh, Carlos, that fool looks like something exploded
    on his face—
Whatever, man. No girls say that.
How do you know?
Because I'm in their bedrooms at night.
Every girl in the world? You're in the bedroom of every
    girl—
Shut up, dude.
I don't even know why we're friends.
I ask myself this every day.
Right?
Every fucking day, D.

CHAPTER NINE

Melanie's not at rehearsal the next day—none of the set crew are. Before rehearsal begins Mrs. McAvoy takes me aside and asks me if I'm okay.

"If you're having a hard time, there's no reason to put yourself through this," she says quietly. "Theater is supposed to be something you enjoy, Damon. I cast you because you seemed right up there, like you understood Othello. But I realize understanding Othello isn't easy and probably doesn't feel easy, and this makes it even harder to play."

Mrs. McAvoy probably thinks I understand Othello because I'm black and have experienced racism, and though both of these things are true, they have so little to do with anything that I feel like laughing. Sure, I've had people look at me funny on the street and in stores. *Crew, really? Theater, really? Black boys don't do that. Straight boys don't do that.* But I don't know anything about living in the kind of society Othello lives in.

Come to think of it, Shakespeare didn't know anything about that either, did he? He wasn't black, probably didn't even know many—perhaps any—black people. Shakespeare didn't understand that side of Othello on any kind of authentic level, but he understood jealousy, obsession, and guilt. He understood grief.

"I can do this," I say. "I want to do this part."

I need to do this part.

Mrs. McAvoy places one hand on my shoulder and squeezes. "All right. Let's do it then. And Damon?"

I glance back at her.

"If you ever need to talk," she says, "you let me know."

The truth is I want to talk to Melanie, even though I don't know exactly what I'd say. But that doesn't feel like an option right now. Not yet.

Everyone tiptoes around me throughout the rehearsal, glancing at me with wary eyes as if I'm some kind of wild animal who might attack at the slightest provocation. It reminds me of the way people looked at me at Carlos's funeral: sidelong glances stolen between eulogies and prayer, everyone apologetic and confused. *There's the boy . . . there's Carlos's friend.* That day I couldn't even cry. The loss was too recent, too raw. The world felt darker, and every touch and hug and comforting word felt like a lie, unfair and undeserved.

> *That's he that was Othello. Here I am. . . .*
> *I am not sorry neither. I'd have thee live,*
> *For in my sense 'tis happiness to die.*

I remember my lines and blocking, but everything blurs during the final scenes. My mind goes milky blank and each motion is studied, a sequence of actions, a line said. When the words are out in the air I'm glad to be rid of them. I collapse in feigned death and don't rise until I feel Lacey's hand on my arm. She's looking down at me, lips curved into a frown.

"You're amazing," Lacey says.

"Thank you," I say, and wish I felt grateful or proud.

The next day is Friday, and we have no rehearsal. I'm about to head home for a long, exciting evening of nothing when my phone buzzes at my hip. I swipe it open to see the text: you got plans?

It's from Tristan. At first I think: *No, too tired*, but then I realize that being around Tristan never makes me feel tired—quite the opposite, in fact, because Tristan has enough energy for ten people. Tristan is exactly the person I need to see.

not really, I text back, and get a smiley face in return, along with: let's do something then. meet me out front, 15 min.

Tristan tumbles out of the school doors a few minutes later, looking quite dapper in his well-fitting gray dress pants and collared shirt.

"You're very dressed up," I say.

"I'm in rebound wear," Tristan says. He hitches his backpack up on his shoulder and frowns. "Let's go to my house."

"Are you sure that's a good—"

"Whatever." Tristan waves me off. "My dad will probably be thrilled I have a guy over I'm not trying to fuck, and you're very butch."

"More butch than Bryan?" I ask.

"Point," Tristan says. "But the truth is nobody's home

most of the time, and my house is bananas. You'll love it."

Tristan's house is indeed bananas. Many of the houses in Tenleytown are modest and small, vestiges of an earlier era when the population was more working class than white collar. These days it skews toward upper middle class, part of D.C.'s gentrification. This basically means families pay more money for the same tiny houses.

Tristan's house, however, is not tiny. It's huge, with giant white columns out front and lots of stacked red brick. When Tristan pushes open the creaky, towering front door he reveals a hallway tiled with what looks to be marble, and everything—*everything*—matches. Beige walls, beige couch, beige curtains. I feel like I am actually standing inside a pair of khakis.

"My mother had money," Tristan says flatly.

"And your dad works for the government?" I ask.

"Senate, a legislative assistant," Tristan says. "He, like, helps make laws or something. But he doesn't make that much money, relatively speaking. Most staffers don't. It's mostly my mother."

"So why do you go to—"

"Public school?" Tristan tosses his backpack onto a chair and gestures for me to do the same. I carefully lower my bag to the floor. "It has a lot do with Melanie's mother, actually."

Tristan leads me into a cavernous kitchen with dark granite countertops and wrenches open the fridge.

"A glass of chardonnay would be lovely, thanks," I jest, and Tristan shoots me an evil look over his shoulder.

"You don't know how many times I've considered that over the last few weeks," Tristan says. "But being drunk doesn't usually work out that well for me. I get really sad or slutty, or slutty, then sad . . . it's a bad situation. In that way I may be more like Michael Cassio than I'd like, to be honest. 'O God, that men should put an enemy in their mouths to steal away their brains!'"

"Sounds dangerous," I say. "I'll have a glass of water if you can spare one."

"I can indeed," Tristan says, and pours me a glass from a Brita filter.

"So what did Melanie's mother have to do with you being in public school?"

"She was a teacher, you know: art. She always taught in the public schools. At first my parents put me in public elementary school because they were like, 'It's little kids and learning their letters, how could they screw it up?' Also, my dad's sort of a cheapskate. But they were going to switch me into private school for middle school and her mother was like, 'You should keep him in public school, it'd be making a statement.'" Tristan closes the fridge door and hops up on a bar stool. "My dad likes making statements."

"That did it, huh?" I say.

"Well, she convinced him it would be a big deal because nobody on the Hill sends their kids to public school," Tristan says. "I didn't complain because it meant I got to stay in school with Melanie."

"Melanie hasn't told me much about her mom," I say.

"I think it's hard for her to talk about it," Tristan says. "She's good at hiding it, but she's in a pretty shitty place right now."

I swallow.

"You and Melanie have been friends forever," I observe.

"Forever and ever." Tristan takes a sip from his own can of Coke.

"She loves you a lot," I say.

Tristan's face softens. "I love her a lot too. She likes you too, you know. A lot."

"I do know," I say. "And I like her. Maybe more than she knows."

"If you're trying to get me to tell you how to make up with her, I can't," Tristan says, fixing me with a steady gaze. "I will say that if you like her, you should tell her. She's really confused on that front right now."

I feel like such an asshole. *I'm sorry*, I want to tell her. *I'm sorry I'm so fucked up. I wish I wasn't. I wish you hadn't been standing so close.*

I can feel my hand shaking. I set down my glass.

"I had this friend," I say. "We were really close, like we never had to explain anything to each other. You know?"

Tristan's eyes are bright. "Yeah, absolutely."

I stop and take a sip of water to have something to do.

"And you had to change schools?" Tristan says. "That sucks, not getting to see him as much."

"He died," I say.

Anytime I say that—and now I've said it exactly twice—it feels wrong. It's so passive. *He died.* Like he just lay down and went to sleep and wasn't around anymore. That's not what it was at all. *He took his own life.* Like Othello. Claimed it. Took it away.

"I'm so sorry," Tristan says.

He rises from the stool and closes the distance between us, wrapping his arms around my shoulders and pulling me into a hug. I'm not usually terribly touchy-feely, but for some reason I don't ever want to say no to Tristan. There's something completely honest about Tristan's affection, like he just wants to give it, and doesn't expect or need anything in return.

"It's not your fault," I say.

"Yeah," Tristan says, "but I'm still sorry."

Me and Tristan hang out until late in the evening, sprawled out on the huge leather couch in the pristine living room, watching horror movies and eating popcorn and getting it everywhere. Tristan is positively gleeful about making a mess. He's also the most entertaining person to watch horror movies with, ever. He makes bitchy comments about everyone's clothes and throws things at the screen when people do dumb stuff like creep down into dark basements by themselves or take long, suspenseful walks through abandoned buildings.

"Why would you do that?" Tristan yelps. "There is practically a sign on the door of that house that says, 'I'm keeping a serial killer in my closet. Ask me how!'"

"I can't tell whether it's more or less stressful watching horror movies with you," I say.

"Yeah, well, I'm really committed," Tristan says around a full mouthful of popcorn, and grins.

I wake up late the next morning and find a new text from Tristan. thanks for protecting me from the monsters, it says, and is followed by a trail of tiny smiley faces. I want to tell Tristan that he's the one protecting me from my monsters, but I think, *Not yet.* Instead I text back: anytime, buddy, and turn my phone off.

I find the bedrooms and the kitchen empty—not everyone is as lazy as I am on Saturday morning, it appears—and leave a note on the kitchen table that says, *Be back later, gone out for walk.—D.*

And then I do just that—I walk. The second my feet touch pavement I know where I have to go.

As long as I allow myself to be afraid, this play will always be my own personal horror movie: scripted, overwrought and filled with inevitable terror. There is only one way for me to own that stage and command it so I can tell Othello's story, and that's for me to feel comfortable on it. This means spending time there, more time than rehearsal provides.

It's a Saturday, but there are sports events and meetings on weekends. The school doors are open when I get there. The auditorium doors are unlocked too. There's nobody inside. My steps echo on the wood as I walk across the stage, pacing it, feeling it under my feet.

Carlos, man. Help me out.

But Carlos isn't there, not even in ghostly form. I'm alone up there on that stage.

I'm alone.

This is what Othello felt too. The isolation, the betrayal, the strangeness.

I wander backstage and stand in front of the backdrop of the castle, staring at the stone walls and spires and turrets. I don't know if this is what a castle in Venice would have looked like back then, but then again, Shakespeare probably wouldn't have known either. The man constantly wrote about foreign lands he'd never seen. Writing about places he'd never been must have been a bit like acting out things he'd never done: The real comes from realizing there is a bit of everything in everything, a drop of everywhere in everywhere else.

I stare at the scenery, narrowing my eyes, and the castle walls smear and blur gray, so gray, they're almost green. The longer I stare, the more the images transform before my eyes, and I wonder if that's what this feeling is: the vertigo that comes from looking at something so long and so hard, I can no longer see it.

The scenery looks different today. I squint. It always looks different, evolving each time I look at it, gaining dimension and color and levels, but this time—

Something has been added. Something is new—

I reach out and trace my fingers over a gnarled tree, branches webbed together like tangled fingers, twisted and twined but beautiful. It looks like the tree in the—

My heartbeat quickens.

No. No, she didn't.

But Melanie did. In one corner of the backdrop, tucked away so it's barely noticeable, is an exact replica of that spot in Rock Creek Park. The spot where I took her when we were just beginning to get to know each other, the spot where she first told me about her mother dying, the spot where I told her that Carlos was dead.

The spot where I first saw Melanie. The spot where—

When you shall these unlucky deeds relate—

I breathe.

That tree has seen a lot of comings and goings. Many people have passed under it, walked by it, spent hours talking near it. I forget that, sometimes: how many people came before.

Melanie. Melanie was one of those people.

I look around the theater, so dusty quiet. There is nothing here but air and silence, and nowhere to go but the one place I always do.

The spot in Rock Creek Park is the same as when we were here a few weeks ago: quietly lovely, branches waving gently with the late afternoon breeze. The sun is low in the sky and it's shadowy under the trees, dark and waning light criss-crossing the mossy green.

There I am. And there she is too.

"Melanie," I say.

Her head jerks up. "Oh. Hi."

"Did we—"

I almost say "make plans," but I know that's not right. This is one of the things I love most about being with Melanie: how wherever we look, we keep finding each other.

I want to touch her. I want to hug her, and I wonder why it's so much harder for me to do that with Melanie than with Tristan. Maybe because both me and Melanie wear such thick, metal-plated armor. No give.

But I'm ready to give.

"I'm sorry," I say. "I'm kind of fucked up."

Melanie looks up, and there's a bit of a smile in her eyes. "You think?"

"A little," I say. I lift my hand and pinch my fingers together, leaving about a half inch of space between them. "This much."

"I think we're both fucked up," Melanie says. "I think . . ."

She pauses, scratching the back of her wrist.

"The scenery," I say. "You painted—"

"Yeah," Melanie says. She gestures up to the tree. "Look close. That's what you said. Right?"

She listened.

She wants to listen.

Carlos left me his pictures. He left me the pictures I put up on my wall, but he left me other ones too.

He left me one picture I will never stop seeing, and it exists only in my mind.

Maybe it needs to exist elsewhere too.

Secrets can be safe, yes. I can keep them shut up inside in boxes fitted with a thousand locks. I can pretend. But what good is that? No matter how many locks I use, they're still there, dormant and waiting, like those photographs in that box. Still there, even if no one ever sees them.

I think of a fortune I received at a Chinese restaurant one week after Carlos died: *Ships in the harbor are safe, but that is not what ships are for.*

"I think you should talk to me about Carlos," she says.

My first thought is, *Oh God, she knows. How does she know?*

But then I realize, no, no. She means—she means my dead friend, the friend I lost. Passive. Because this is what she already knows.

I did not lose him, and I do not want to let him go.

"Carlos killed himself," I say.

Melanie gazes at me with wide eyes. "He—Carlos *killed himself?*"

I can't say it again. I sit down on a mossy tree stump and bury my head in my hands.

I can feel Melanie beside me, her hand flat between my shoulder blades. "Damon, please keep talking. Please?"

I think of all the times, in this spot, that I've come to talk to Carlos, to ask him questions. But Carlos never cared that much about words. He wanted pictures. He wanted it right in front of him: no filters, no lies.

But pictures can hide too, push something out of the frame, edit it out. Pictures are puzzle pieces, and sometimes they don't fit together. Sometimes they are just pieces, fragments without a frame, and sometimes we look and we don't see.

"We were supposed to hang out that night," I say. "But he called me and he was acting all weird, talking about how he was dizzy, how he couldn't see, and I—I tried to find him. I went everywhere I could think to go, and I kept calling him, and I got through but he wouldn't tell me where he was, and then I lost the signal, and when I finally got it back . . ."

I stop. This. This is the part of the story I've never told, never said out loud. This is the part of the conversation I've never even had with ghost Carlos, because I was afraid.

"I went to his house and I found this stuff in his room," I say. "His camera and a box of photos, and I took them. Carlos used to say: *Photos are stories, man, they're what we leave behind.* And I'd say that was morbid, that he shouldn't talk like that, that we were young and shouldn't be thinking about our . . . legacy or whatever. He'd get angry, tell me I didn't know what the fuck I was talking about."

I sigh. I can feel Melanie's fingertips press into the back of my neck.

"He was right," I say. "I didn't know what the fuck I was talking about."

I'm silent for a moment, my thoughts melting together in my mind.

"But when you tried to call again, you couldn't get through?" she prods.

"No, I did get through," I say. "I had all this shit going through my head, crisis training and first aid and I don't even know what else, and all he said was, 'I'm in the park, come to the park.' And I knew. There was this place we used to go sometimes after crew practice. It was beautiful, quiet and green and the opposite of the city and—"

"It was here," Melanie says suddenly. "You came here."

Now. Now she knows.

A bird flies overhead, its cry hollow and sad. I can hear the whir of traffic. No matter where you go, other people are never that far away.

I take in a deep breath.

"I went to the park," I say. "It was raining, and I ran and ran, and I tried to keep talking to him, tried to keep him on the line. He kept drifting in and out, saying crazy stuff like, 'I don't need this, I don't need you, I don't need you.' It was like talking to a wall, because he didn't give a shit what I said."

I close my eyes. I can see Carlos slumped against that tree, arms folded across his chest. It was so dark, I couldn't see anything but his outline, the shape of him gray over black. I ran to him and crouched down and pulled him up, but Carlos was limp. His whole body was limp and his clothes were soaked through. I pressed a hand to this throat, felt his too-slow thud of a pulse.

Fuck you, Damon, he'd whispered. *Fuck you, man.*

Carlos, stay with me. Stay with me, please, just—

Like at that point Carlos still had a choice.

I'm sorry, Carlos said.

What are you sorry for? I asked. *Don't be sorry.*

I will never forget holding him like that, the rain turning my clothes to ice against my skin. My shoes were covered in mud. I kept whispering, over and over, *Stay with me, man. Stay with me.* But I knew he couldn't hear me.

"When the police came, he was still alive," I whisper. "He was still alive in the ambulance on the way to the hospital, but he was unconscious. He was still alive at the hospital, but not for very long. They came out and they said he'd taken too many pills, that they'd been in his system too long."

"Damon," Melanie murmurs.

"And I keep thinking I could've done something," I say. "Gotten there quicker. Read the fucking signs, you know? But then some days I'm so angry at him, I want to kick his ass, and that makes me so angry at myself, I want to cry. I get up on that stage and I do that death scene and I see Desdemona and I see Carlos like he looked in this park. And I'm Othello, but Carlos was Othello too. Carlos made that decision—*for in my sense 'tis happiness to die*—and he planned it and he went to this very spot and then he called me to come find him. He knew I'd come for him like I'd come ten thousand times before, every time he was in trouble. He made me part of his plan. He knew I'd take his fucking camera. He knew me so fucking well, but I don't think I ever knew him."

"No," Melanie says. "No, you knew him. You knew where to find him. You were the only person who did."

Melanie

Your hand, on my arm, in the hospital, was so cold. I kept thinking: Where did all your fire go?

CHAPTER TEN

begin to cry. I can't help it.

Damon moves forward, arm encircling my shoulders. He pulls me closer, and then I'm pressed against his chest, shaking.

"Oh God, I'm so sorry," he murmurs, and the words ghost across my scalp, disappearing into my hair. I'm pretty sure I'm still crying, but all I feel is the pendant of his gold necklace making an indentation in my cheek, his arms and his heat and his spicy boy smell all around me.

"Why are you sorry?" I say. My voice doesn't sound like my own.

"I didn't mean to—I didn't want to make you upset," Damon says.

"But it is upsetting," I say. "You're allowed to be upset about things that are upsetting."

I can feel Damon shaking, and I wonder if he's crying too. Crying is never something you want to do alone. I've done a lot of crying alone.

"It's never okay when somebody dies, Damon," I say. "Never."

I think of how I'd feel if Tristan killed himself: It would be like someone had ripped my skin off and left me raw and exposed. How guilty I'd feel, how useless, how afraid.

I look into Damon's eyes and know he feels all of this too, and he's been feeling it by himself.

"I'm not going to say I'm sorry," I say. "I don't think that would help."

"It wouldn't," Damon says. "No offense."

"I won't say it's not your fault either," I say, "because I'm sure you've heard that a lot."

Damon nods. I can see his throat work as he swallows.

"I'm only going to say that I think you're wonderful," I say, "and I have that picture of Carlos you gave me still, on my dresser, and I'm pretty sure—" I stop to catch my breath. "I'm pretty sure he thought you were wonderful too."

Damon's arms tighten around my shoulders. His eyes are glittering and wet. He looks up at the sky. It's almost dark and getting chilly. I'm shivering. I didn't even notice. Damon takes off his jacket and wraps it around my shoulders.

"It's okay that you feel like this," I say. "The way you feel right now—it's okay. It's okay to be angry, and sad, and feel helpless. You don't have to hide it."

Love your grief, the grief book said.

Suddenly I think I understand.

Damon's face is so soft and sad.

"Let's go somewhere," he says, and when he gets up, I follow.

Damon doesn't talk about what I said, or what he said, or what I didn't say, or what he didn't say. Instead he leads me out of the park, onto the sidewalk, into a Best Buy. There's something comforting about the glaring, jarring, twitching rhythm of all those flickering TVs, the noisy stereos, the hum of random noise. We wander aimlessly up and down the aisles, and he shows me different kinds of cameras—the one he has now that used to be Carlos's, the one he wants for his birthday. We discuss shutter speed and Photoshop and Damon's eyes light up when he talks about photographing flowers and trees, trying to get each blossom to stand out, to be able to see every wrinkle and vein of the leaves and petals.

We grab coffee at Starbucks and sit for a while at the wooden tables, listening to smooth jazz and sipping caffeinated beverages. He seems to be waiting for me to speak, but I don't really want to talk. I don't think he wants to either. The coffee shop whirs all around us, the sounds of chattering voices, the purr and grumble of the espresso machines, the chiming of the opening and closing doors. Each customer brings a puff of winter air in with them as they enter or leave. We share the silence. It's November now, the beginning of the end of the year.

Over the last few months I've spent a lot of time looking at Damon Lewis, admiring the slender curve of his wrists or the swell of his biceps or the Crayola green of his eyes. But I can't help feeling, sitting here in this coffee shop, the world going on around us, that I'm seeing him for the first time.

We walk back to Damon's house. No one is home, and everything is clean and neat. Damon leads me up the stairs to his bedroom. There are still boxes stacked in one corner, and his laptop is the only object on his desk. I stare at his walls for several minutes, taking in the pale blue paint covered with a massive web of photographs, people and places and things. I stare until the colors begin to swirl and blur.

"Did you take—" I start to say.

"No," Damon says. "Carlos."

My chest hurts.

"I want you to have this," Damon says, and holds out one photo that's not on his wall.

My own face stares back at me, eyes rimmed with messy black, cheeks flushed a milky pink.

"Oh my God," I whisper.

"I took this," he says, "before I first met you. Over the summer. You were—"

"—in Rock Creek Park," I say.

"I should have asked," Damon says. "But that's the thing about taking photos. You wait and the moment's gone."

I take in a deep breath. I could freak out right now, knowing Damon took this picture before we even spoke. But I think I understand why he did it.

Damon looked at me and he saw. He saw what everybody else had been missing, and I didn't even have to say it.

I remember how he reached out to touch the scar near my eye the night we kissed on that rooftop. *I like it*, he'd said. *You're demented*, I'd replied. He was framing me, trying to see me and everything that makes me who I am. Scars included.

It should make me feel self-conscious, knowing this, knowing how closely he looks. But now I know something about Damon that can't be seen too.

I examine the photograph—my shoulders curved, eyes downcast, hands bunched at my sides. I seem so compact, pinched and tight, closed off. I look closer: Behind me stands a tree, gnarled and old, branches reaching out like open arms.

"That's the same spot where—"

"Yeah," Damon says, and lowers his eyes.

Wherever I look, there you are.

The photo feels slippery in my hand, as malleable as memory.

Sometimes I wake up and can't remember which side of my mother's face had more freckles, the left or the right. The details seem unimportant, but they're everything. They make something real and special and itself.

I watch Damon's face, the way it shifts and settles.

"You said Carlos left you the camera and the photographs," I say. "Are the ones on your walls the ones he left you?"

"There are more," Damon says.

He crouches down and unearths a brown cardboard box from under the bed. He lifts off the lid and inside I can see piles of images, layer upon layer. He holds out the box to me.

Outside a strong wind pushes through the trees. Damon's bedroom window is open just a crack, and the breeze tickles the hairs on my forearms. I take the box and sit down on the edge of Damon's bed.

I lift out a shot of the Mall in springtime, trees green and heavy, cherry blossoms floating in the air like huge, dry snowflakes.

"These are beautiful," I say.

"Some are beautiful," Damon says. "Some aren't."

He reaches into the box and takes out a photo of a homeless woman, squatting down by the side of a building, surrounded by dirty blankets and plastic bags filled with cans and bottles. The bottles glitter in the sun, green and blue, shiny red crumpled Coke cans and silver and black containers for energy drinks. But the woman looks old and gray and tired, fading into the concrete facade behind her.

"That's amazing," I say.

"I know." Damon scratches behind his ear. "I never knew Carlos thought about—I mean, we talked about serious stuff. But I never knew he saw poverty like that. That he cared, I guess. There are a lot of photos like that one in here. He took these ones at this housing project in Anacostia, and—"

Damon pauses, rummaging through the box and locating a picture of a young boy, tucked into a dark stairwell. His clothes are too big on his thin frame, and he looks exhausted, as if he hasn't slept in days. On the wall above his head are two words etched in spray paint: *OUR FUTURE*.

I suck in a breath. I can feel this photo, as if it's reached out and punched me in the stomach. There are so many things I know are there, in the corners and out of my line of vision, hidden in plain sight. But I never see them unless someone makes me look.

"I'll never know if he really wanted to die," Damon says. "He took pills. A lot of the time pills don't even work. He had all this time to change his mind. I feel like maybe he did change his mind, because Carlos was like that, you know? He'd be all gung-ho about some crazy thing, and then later he'd be like, 'That was stupid, what was I thinking?' But this time—"

He stops. I reach over the box and find Damon's hand, lacing our fingers together. He looks up, and he doesn't smile, but the tightness around his eyes softens.

"We don't have to talk about this," Damon says. "This is depressing, and it's not like you need more things to—"

"I don't think this is depressing," I say. "This is Carlos's life. This is what he wanted you to see, Damon. This is who he was, or who he thought he was, anyway. I feel like when people die they leave behind all these clues about themselves. My mom left her studio. My dad moved everything into the basement, but he left it exactly the way it was when she was alive. He hasn't touched it since. At first I thought it was because he couldn't face it, like he just couldn't deal, but then I realized that studio is her, to him—it's where he can still see her, still connect to her, you know? For me too—when I'm there I feel her there too."

Damon grips my hand more tightly, and I don't pull away. I place my palm on his back. He's warm, T-shirt damp with sweat. He smells like trees.

"We should look at these photos," I say. "Together."

Damon lifts his head. His eyes are a dark watery green, like the Atlantic Ocean under a cloudy sky.

"Okay," he says.

We examine the photos one by one. Sometimes we make up stories to go with them. Sometimes Damon stops and stares and doesn't say anything for long, painful minutes. Watching him, I know there are stories I will never know, stories that belong only to Damon and Carlos, only to Damon now.

"This one," I say, holding up a photo of Damon dressed in a collared shirt and slacks, sleeves pushed up above his elbows. "Where did he take this?"

"Play rehearsal," Damon says. "At Gate, last year, we did an August Wilson play. Carlos took some photos for the newspaper review of the production."

There are other photos of Damon underneath them—so many. Damon in the play. Damon doing crew. With his parents. Alone. All of them are beautiful, spontaneous, real. Never posed. Damon never seemed to know Carlos was taking them.

"This, all the photos he took of you," I say softly. "It's not that he got your good side. It's like he didn't think you had a bad one."

Damon looks down at his hands. I can see the way two nails on his left hand are broken, skin dry at the knuckles.

"He was wrong," Damon says.

"He loved you, Damon," I say.

Damon's face is shuttered closed.

"He didn't tell me," Damon says, so softly I have to strain to hear him.

I think, for a moment, that Damon's repeating what he said before. *I keep thinking I could've done something.* But then I realize: *oh.*

There's a reason Damon keeps these photos in a box.

He knew me so fucking well, but I don't think I ever knew him.

"I wish—I don't know," Damon says.

I wait.

"After he died I couldn't even look at the photos," Damon says. "For weeks I kept them in that box under my bed, but I knew they were there, you know? Just sitting there, waiting for me to look at them."

Damon swallows. He still won't look at me.

"One night I couldn't sleep," he continues, "and I took out the box and I looked through them and I realized—Carlos was always trying to cover up anything too emotional with a joke, or he'd get pissed off and get mean or change the subject. He was a master at that, at avoiding getting too deep. He could be evasive as hell. But it was all so clear in those photos, all these pictures he took of me but never showed me."

I wait, but he doesn't say anything. His hands are shaking.

"What, Damon?" I ask. "What was so clear?"

Damon takes in a deep breath and lets it go all at once.

"The way he looked at me," he says.

235

I feel the tears coming on again, hot in my throat. I swallow them down.

Photographs are what we leave behind, Carlos had said. So he'd left his for Damon, his legacy in a box: what he didn't know how to tell Damon, what felt like too much to say out loud. He'd left them there for Damon to see.

But photographs aren't all we leave behind. Not photographs, not letters, not drawings or paintings, not houses or cars or money or clothes.

People are what we leave behind.

Of one who loved not wisely but too well. Carlos was so brave and yet so afraid. I wish, even now, even though I never knew him, that I could just sit with him and hold his hand and say, *It will get better. It may never be perfect, but it will be okay.*

But I can't do that for Carlos, or for my mom.

I can do it for Damon.

"I know I said I wouldn't say that it's not your fault," I say. "But it's not your fault if you didn't feel the same way he—"

"I know," Damon says, his voice soft. "I know, but it doesn't matter, does it? Like—whether it's my fault or not. This is the way I feel now, and he's still gone."

She's still gone.

I want to say what everybody says: *I'm sorry.* It's automatic, easy.

But I don't.

"I wish I could make this better," I say.

Damon squeezes my hand.

When he speaks, his voice is hoarse.

"Oh, Melanie," he says. "Trust me, you do."

On impulse I lean in and kiss Damon's cheek—just a brush of the lips, just so he can feel the contact. When I pull away he's staring down at me, eyes tracing my face.

"I think people should see these," I say. "People who are not us."

Damon blinks, slowly, and I can tell he's never considered this.

"Speak of me as I am," he whispers.

I stare at him for a moment, allowing the puzzle pieces to move and slide around until they fit.

"Yeah," I say. "Exactly."

We spend hours poring over the photos. Downstairs the house comes to life with the sounds of dinner being made, but neither of us are enticed by the prospect of food. When Damon's mom comes upstairs to tell him to come to dinner, I stay quiet and Damon calls through the door that he's not feeling well. It's not exactly a lie.

Shadows climb the walls and we fall asleep together, photographs scattered across the bed.

I wake in the middle of the night because the shades are still open, moonlight streaming through the glass. It's cold, and I'm bundled up in blankets, pulled up to my chin. I don't want to close the windows because I like the feel of the cool air on my face, smelling of lit fireplaces and pine and approaching winter.

Damon is so warm beside me, arm snug around my waist. I can feel him breathe against my neck, and it's so good. Everything is so good.

Should it feel this good? Should it feel this good when they are gone?

"Hey," Damon whispers.

"Hey," I say, and he brings his hand up and brushes my hair out of my eyes.

"You okay?" he asks.

I swallow.

"I miss her," I whisper. "I really, really miss her."

I can feel him inhale, then exhale slowly.

"I bet she misses you too," Damon murmurs.

"Do you think it ever . . ."

"Goes away?" Damon says. "No. I don't. I think when you love somebody, the grief's forever."

I close my eyes and try to breathe. I feel Damon tracing my face with his fingertips, soft, slow.

"You know you can tell me about her," Damon says. "Whenever you want to, I'm here. I want to listen."

I exhale. Tears slip down my cheeks.

I can be a mess. I am allowed to be a mess.

Let yourself be seen.

"My mom left me this letter," I say.

Damon's eyes focus. I feel like the words are caught in my throat.

"What did the letter say?" he says.

Everything, I want to say.

I wish I could write her back. I would say: *You're right, Mom. You were kind of a lot, always. Sometimes it felt like there was no way for me to be seen because all anyone could ever see was you.*

But even when I wanted that—when I wanted things to be different, when I wanted to be different—I never wanted it like this.

I never wanted it without you.

I say, "She said that I was beautiful and talented."

"True," Damon interrupts, and gives me a dorky smile when I narrow my eyes. "Sorry. Please continue."

"She said that I should be myself and let people see me. She said—"

I stop, because I can feel the tears coming faster.

He says, "You don't have to—"

"No," I say. "I do. I do have to."

I take in a deep breath.

"She said," I say, "that I'm not alone."

"You're not alone," he whispers. "You're not, Melanie."

Damon wraps me up in his arms, holding me so close, it's like he's all around me.

I like to think my mother exists somewhere between here and now and elsewhere, and in that place she sits back and watches the living screw everything up. Sometimes she laughs and sometimes she cries, but mostly she rests and hangs out and is comfortable and peaceful in a way she couldn't be while she was alive because she always had something to do, somewhere to be, someone to satisfy.

I don't know how these things work, but I hope that wherever she is, there's a lot of good music: the kind she can dance to, move her hips in little circles, *swish swish*, flick out her wrists and throw her head back and laugh. I have to believe Etta James is there too, singing her face off in heaven, because a heaven without Etta would be no heaven at all. Mom would like that, to be somewhere she could get her groove on all the time, with infinite dance partners and drinks for all and a beat that never stops.

Maybe she can dance and paint too, fill the world with her colors, spread them everywhere, all across the sky, spill them on the ground, puff them out into the air. Maybe someday I will take all those crusty cans of paint out of the basement and bring them upstairs and find somewhere in my room to put them. I'll draw and I'll paint and somehow she'll see what I make, wherever she is, however she's able to see.

I'll keep her close. I'll keep her close and I won't forget and she'll be here.

She'll stay.

I wake in the morning wrapped around Damon, head tucked under his chin, using his chest as a pillow. I stay still for a few moments, rising and falling with his measured breaths.

"Damon," I murmur. "I should go home."

"Mmm," he snuffles, and shudders into waking. "I don't wanna get up."

"You don't have to get up," I say, "but if I don't go home, my dad's going to call the police."

He blinks his eyes open. They're blurry from sleep but still that same vivid shifting green, the color of trees, leaves, plants that grow.

"I want to see you later," he says.

"I want to see you later too," I say.

"Like, later today," Damon says. "You know, I want to take your picture. For real this time."

"Not creepy stalker-style?" I say, smiling, and Damon flushes.

"More of a candid photo shoot," Damon says.

"Sad," I say. "I sort of like the idea of having my very own paparazzi."

He smiles, a sleepy twitch of the lips, and I kiss him before he can say anything else.

"Thank you," I say, and I know he knows what I'm thanking him for.

DAMON

Carlos, man, if you're watching . . .
Watch me now.

CHAPTER ELEVEN

I wake a second time on Sunday morning to the sound of my parents thumping around downstairs and the smell of coffee brewing in the kitchen. I roll over in bed and burrow under the sheets, seeking lost warmth. Melanie is gone. I knew that she would be, but it still feels strange: My body keeps trying to fill the space she left behind.

There are photographs everywhere, tucked between the sheets and inside my pillowcase and on the windowsill and all over the floor. I get out of bed and stumble around the room collecting them, shaking them out of fabric and tugging them from the cracks they've fallen into, and stack them together.

I lift the camera from its place on the desk to check its battery power. Stuck to the base is another photograph. I peel it off and stare at it. It's black and white, a photograph of only a silhouette, shadows on snow. The shape reminds me of a chalk outline, the contours etched into the sidewalk at a murder scene. I squint—it looks familiar. I remember:

You never take pictures of yourself, man, I said as we tripped through the snow, white crunching beneath our dirty boots. *No self-portraits?*

Self-portraits are boring, Carlos scoffed. *Nothing to see here.*

But a few minutes later he'd stopped and brought the camera up and snapped a single shot. I thought he was just taking a photo of the snow, but now I know I was wrong.

Nothing to see here. I lower the photograph to the desk. That was it, wasn't it? Carlos saw so much around him, so much pain, so much beauty. But he couldn't see his real self. All he saw were shadows in the snow, borders and outlines and darkness and nothing inside.

When he turned the camera on himself, he was afraid of what he saw.

I can't put these back in that box. Melanie's right, I can't keep hiding them.

I can't keep your secrets, man.

Let them breathe, D. Let them go.

I shiver. I turn in a slow circle, but the room is empty.

My mind conjures up an image of the scenery from the play, those high castle walls, and outside them that lonely tree: Melanie's one-man forest. On that stage, I feel like that tree, isolated and afraid. But I don't have to.

Carlos didn't have to feel—

I drop the photos onto my desk and grab my phone. When I text Melanie I get an almost instant response.

i like the way you think. come by the restaurant later.

Melanie's working the dinner shift. The restaurant smells like lime juice and grease. I nearly run into Macho while coming back from the bathroom. He is currently throwing a very pronounced hissy fit.

"How is anyone supposed to work around here with all

this nonsense going on?" he asks, flailing his arms. "Crazy busy, crazy people . . ."

I duck, and he careens into the kitchen. Through the open kitchen door I see Melanie nearly collide with him, deftly avoiding getting smacked in the face at the last moment with a quick swerve. She dumps some dishes into a vat of dirty dishwater and exits the kitchen with haste. I take a seat at the table with Tristan, who's studying the script in his lap and idly carding his fingers through his hair.

"Hey, waitress!" I call out when Melanie walks by. She sticks out her tongue and keeps going, but returns a couple minutes later bearing food.

"I know you're going to want fries, so here's your fries, dumbass," she says, sliding the plate piled high with steaming potatoes over to me, then drops another plate onto the table next to Tristan. "And your burger, idiot."

"Do you always talk to the customers this way?" I ask. "I'm shocked and appalled."

"The service in this place used to be so excellent too," Tristan complains.

"Oh ho ho, Tweedle-dum and Tweedle-dumber," Melanie snorts. "Talk to me some other time when you're not eating for free."

I grin up at her.

"We love you, Melanie," I say. "We kid because we love."

"I don't know, I just wanted a burger," Tristan inserts. "Running lines makes a man hungry."

"Hell Week," I lament. "Aptly named."

"As if he's even stressed," Tristan says with a roll of the eyes. "He's had the lines memorized since the second day of rehearsal."

"I like the play," I say, affronted.

"Hey, as enchanting as this conversation is, I gotta go, y'know, like, work and stuff?" Melanie gestures to the busy restaurant. "So you boys enjoy your meal, okay?"

She turns to go, but I grasp her wrist.

"Later, right?" I ask. "You promised."

She nods, eyes suddenly dark. "Yeah. Yeah, I promised."

A couple hours later we're shivering outside the door of the Hamilton gym, Melanie making a big show of blowing on her hands and then rubbing them together to keep warm. Melanie is still wearing her work clothes, and she smells sweet and a little sweaty. I want to lean in and lick her.

"I have to say I'm a little alarmed at how bad the security is at this school," Melanie says. "Where are the beefy guards? My history textbook is in there. What if it got stolen? That would be tragic. It's only ten years out of date! It might be a collector's item."

"You might never know who really shot JFK," I say.

"Please don't ever get Tristan started on that subject," Melanie says, twisting the bobby pin until the lock clicks open. "If you pretend you're listening, he stops eventually, but it takes a while. Pro tip."

"I will keep this in mind," I say.

"So what's the plan here?" Melanie asks as we cross the gym and walk down the hallway, shoes squeaking on recently mopped linoleum. We push through the theater doors, walk down the aisle, and shove our way past the curtains backstage.

The set is all there, painted to look like castle walls, surrounded by trees.

I hold out the cardboard box.

"I thought we'd put them up over the gray space," I say. "Just kind of—fill it in."

"Make the castle a little less lonely?" Melanie says.

"Yeah," I say. "I just . . . I want them near me when I'm up there."

I want him near me.

When I look into Melanie's eyes, I know I don't have to say it.

"I think this is going to be awesome," Melanie says.

"I hope so," I say.

"Also, as a bonus," Melanie says, "Calvin is going to lose his mind."

"Oh man," I say. "That is *such* a bonus."

I open the box of photographs, shaking it until every last one is scattered across the floor. "Okay," I say. "Here goes."

Melanie places her hand on my wrist—gentle, there—and squeezes.

We work at it for a few minutes, pasting the photos into corners and around set pieces.

We're so involved in what we're doing that we don't hear the footsteps.

"What are you doing? Who is that?"

Mrs. McAvoy emerges from the darkness of the theater. *Shit.*

It's possible we didn't really think this through.

"Damon, Melanie?" she says. She trips up the steps to the stage and looks at us, bewildered. "What—"

"I can explain," Melanie and I say in unison.

She raises her eyebrows. "Well, one of you better."

"It was my idea," I say. "I just—I thought it needed some filling in."

This is such BS, and I can tell Mrs. McAvoy isn't buying it. The woman is not an idiot. She leans in, adjusting her glasses, and examines the photographs.

"These are beautiful," she says.

I feel proud hearing that. Proud of Carlos. And so sad he's not here to hear it.

"It's very striking, what you and Melanie have done," Mrs. McAvoy says slowly. "But I would have appreciated if you'd asked me first before you added your photographs like this. You know that wasn't part of the original set design, and it's very late to make changes—"

"The photos aren't mine," I correct her. "They were taken by a friend. Carlos."

Mrs. McAvoy tilts her head to one side. "Does he go to Hamilton?"

"He's not—no, he doesn't," I say. "Carlos is dead."

Her face pales in that way people's often do when confronted with death during an otherwise polite conversation. It's helplessness, writ large.

"Oh," she says, her voice soft.

I can see her scrambling. It always feels unfair to put people in this position, because there is no right thing to say. No magic words.

She lifts her eyes to mine.

"Damon," she says, "does this have anything to do with why it's been so hard for you to rehearse the death scenes in the play?"

My throat tightens. I can feel Melanie watching me.

I breathe.

If you ever need to talk, Mrs. McAvoy had said, *you let me know.*

I keep thinking that nobody sees, but they do.

They do.

"Yes," I say. "Yes, it has something to do with that."

She nods, and her face softens. She doesn't ask anything else. She doesn't push.

"I understand why you want to put these up," she says, "but I think maybe they don't belong behind you like this. It's hard for others to truly see them when they're part of the set, and I think people should get to see them. What would you think about us displaying them in the hallway instead? Make it sort of an exhibit to honor him? I think that display of photographs of sports teams has been up there quite a while."

"It has," Melanie says. "I'm pretty sure it's been up there since the beginning of time."

Mrs. McAvoy smiles. "I can talk to some people about moving it at the very least, then."

My heartbeat speeds up. I can do this. I can make Carlos's mark. I can leave the kinds of marks Carlos left all over me: marks, lines, or brushstrokes, permanent and real, but not scars.

"Mrs. McAvoy?" I hear Melanie say.

"Yes, Melanie?"

"It's just, I think if we're going to have an exhibit—I mean, not that Carlos's photos aren't amazing and great, but . . . maybe we should let other people contribute too." Melanie's eyes flick down to the floor. "To honor the other people we've lost."

Mrs. McAvoy looks overwhelmed, but not upset. "Do you think there are other people who would want to contribute?"

"Yes," Melanie says. "Me."

Melanie and I walk home together. She holds my hand and it feels good to have her so close. We don't talk, and by the time we get to her house I feel full to the brim with things I don't know how to say.

"Does it bother you?" Melanie says suddenly. "I mean, would you rather that it just be Carlos's stuff in the exhibit?"

"Of course not," I say, squeezing her hand. "Melanie— God, no. The more the—well, not the merrier, maybe, but—"

"The less alone," Melanie says.

"Exactly," I say.

I kiss her. It's soft and light, and when I pull away, she's smiling.

I wake up the morning of opening night and spend some quality time staring at the ceiling, letting the lines scroll before my eyes like ticker tape. It's never been the lines that have been the problem, though. Memorizing is easy. Forgetting is harder.

My phone buzzes on my nightstand. I reach out and flip it open.

don't stress out, Melanie's message says. you're going to be fantastic.

I smile. I'm about to text her again when my phone vibrates.

etta said it best: trust in me in all you do/have the faith i have in you.

I text her back: you ready for the show?

I don't mean the play, and this Melanie knows.

It takes a few minutes before she texts me back.

i don't know, she says. maybe.

it's ok to feel whatever you feel, I text her back. someone rly smart told me that.

I'm getting dressed when I get her reply.

flattery will get you everywhere, mr. lewis, she says, and then, a moment later: at least at the end of the night, we'll be together.

I get to school a couple hours before the play is scheduled to start and find much of the cast and crew already there.

They're not gathered backstage, though. They're in the hallway in front of the theater, where we put up Carlos's photos.

I didn't put them all up. I chose the ones that felt the most like his, the most like him. Some of my family, of me, of places in the city I know he loved. The ones he took in Anacostia. His shadow on the snow, Carlos and his visual echo.

Carlos, unedited. Even the parts that are hard for me to look at. Even the parts that took me a long time to see.

Next to the photos I wrote out a card that says: *Photos taken by Carlos Antonio Remedios Ruiz-Gutierrez, 1999–2016.*

You have the longest name in the world, I used to tease him.

He'd shove me and say, *You know what they say, the bigger the name, the bigger the—* and I'd put my hand over his mouth before he could finish.

My eyes skim up. I see that above the card with his name is the picture I gave Melanie, the one I took of him all those months ago. Carlos and that devil grin.

It hits me, so hard and fast, I have to remind myself to keep breathing.

Carlos was that boy drugged out and cursing me in the park, pushing me away and pulling me back in again. He was desperate and secretive and he will always, always be a mystery to me, an unknown, the *x* I can never solve for.

But he was also this.

Sometimes he was happy.

"Is it okay?" I hear Melanie say, and realize she is standing beside me.

"It's great," I say, and I mean it.

My eyes drift. Next to the photographs are a series of drawings. They're many versions of the same woman as she gets thinner and thinner, her rounded features growing sharper and sharper. She is beautiful but also gets more frightening as the drawings progress, as her profile becomes more stark, as she fades.

"These are incredible, Melanie," I say, because they are.

She's dying, I realize.

"This is my mom," Melanie says.

This is the first time I've ever seen pictures of Melanie's mom. Melanie has her eyes. Not just the shape and color, but something about the look in them. The wisdom. The understanding.

"God, Melanie," I whisper, and wrap my arm around her waist and hold her close. She is stiff, at first, but slowly she relaxes, her body melting against mine.

"She's beautiful," I say, and I can feel Melanie take in a deep breath, then let it go.

"Melanie?" I hear behind me, and there's Max, looking more serious than I've ever seen her look. "Sorry, I overheard. This is your mom?"

"Yeah," Melanie says, and I release her from my embrace. She stays close.

Max glances at the card next to the pictures, which reads: *Dana Marie Ellis, 1968–2016.*

"She just died this year," Max says, her eyes wide. "She was young."

"Yeah," Melanie says, and I can see her swallow.

Max reaches out and wraps her hand around Melanie's wrist.

"My dad," she says, "died a couple years ago. It was the hardest thing I've ever had to go through."

Melanie looks so sad. "I'm so—"

"Don't say you're sorry," Max says. "Please?"

Max moves forward and catches Melanie up in a hug. When they separate she says, "Do you think maybe I can like—bring something in and add to this? My dad loved music, and—"

"Absolutely," I say. "Anyone is welcome."

"I made a blanket for my grandmother after she died," Tristan says. He's standing a few feet away, his eyes not moving from Melanie's drawings. "It's kind of ugly, but—"

"I didn't know that," Melanie says.

"Yeah, well, you don't know everything about me," Tristan says, tossing her a smile. Melanie wraps her hand around his wrist and holds on, keeping him in a loose grip.

"It doesn't have to be pretty," Melanie says, and I know she means his blanket, but maybe she means all of this.

All of what's left behind when someone is gone.

Maybe it could have been different with Carlos—not just if I'd known, but if he had. If he'd known he wasn't alone in all this. If he'd known that if he'd reached out, other people would have reached back, would have held his hand.

Let's do this, I can see Carlos shouting, standing with his feet wedged between the bars of the bridge, arms spread wide, leaning forward so much that my breath caught. *Let's show the world who we are.*

When Melanie sneaks backstage to find me before the show, I'm half dressed in tailored dark purple-striped pants and an undershirt, caught somewhere between the Moorish prince and myself.

"Hey, look who it is," I say, and grab her around her waist and yank her forward, pulling her into a kiss.

"Oh, gross, gross," Tristan says, pushing past us carrying a couple of swords. "Backstage PDA is so tacky."

"Shut up, Tristan," I say, and he pokes me in the side with one of the prop swords.

"Hey, look, I get that Melanie is like your real-life Desdemona," Tristan says, "but in case you've forgotten? That did not turn out so well. I'm just sayin'."

I look down at Melanie.

"Melanie's not my Desdemona," I murmur. "She's my Melanie."

Tristan pretends to retch, and narrowly escapes being kicked in the kneecaps by scampering into the wings.

"You're an idiot," Melanie tells me, and I smirk.

"Yeah, but you like me," I tease. "You like me a lot."

This time Melanie kisses me, pressing her lips to the corner of my mouth.

"I do kinda like you," she says. "Sometimes."

I snort, fingers curving around her waist and lingering.

"Break a leg," she says.

"I might," I say, grinning. "I heard the set construction's a little shoddy."

Melanie rolls her eyes and makes as if to leave, but I grab her arm.

"Thank you," I whisper, and Melanie's eyes soften.

"You don't need to thank me for anything," she says.

I hold her gaze. In my mind I'm circling Melanie, looking through the viewfinder and seeing her there—no smoke and mirrors, no set pieces, no memorized lines, no false fronts. I think of her breath against my face and my hands in her hair and my lips cold and dry against her cheek.

I think of the way she holds my hand, fingers threaded through and thumb stroking along my skin, skimming, light.

You're not alone. You're not alone. You're not alone.

"I'll be there when it's over," Melanie says, and then she's gone.

Under Othello's skin is still a frightening place to be.

Who can control his fate? 'Tis not so now.
Be not afraid, though you do see me weaponed.

Here is my journey's end, here is my butt,
And very sea-mark of my utmost sail.

Onstage, I never falter. I understand my lines and my blocking. I understand Othello. I understand Othello's pride and his anger, his straightforward thinking and his naive and eternal trust in others. I understand his way of speaking, unusually direct for Shakespeare, particularly striking in a play where so few say what they mean. I understand his love for Desdemona, his soldier's resolve, his jealousy and his irrational fears.

I understand this play about jealousy, this play about grief, this play about loving someone the world doesn't want you to love.

When act 5, scene 2 rolls around, I am so exhausted, I am beyond exhaustion, situated in that strange middle space where everything is distorted from weariness. I turn to deliver my final speech, and have a sudden flash of Carlos and me together in a crew boat, sweaty and laughing. I remember:

You dickwad, when he says stroke you pull.

That's what I was doing, asshole. It's not my fault if you suck at this.

If I suck? If I—

I shoved Carlos then, and Carlos shoved me back, Carlos saying, *Are you afraid of me? You are, aren't you? You scared of all this?*

I shoved him back, laughing: *Yeah, Carlos, you are just too much man for me to handle—*

When we got out of the boat, Carlos slung his arm around my shoulders, pulling me close and whispering in my ear, *Teamwork, Lewis. We work together, we're unstoppable.*

Goddamn right, I said, and my mouth felt like it couldn't stretch wide enough to contain my smile.

It hurts, having that camera and not having Carlos.

We never took enough pictures together.

I am so sorry for that, man.

But I don't need those photos behind me, I realize. I've got him with me all the time.

"I pray you, in your letters," I begin, and my voice, as Othello's, shakes, "when you shall these unlucky deeds relate, speak of me as I am. Nothing extenuate, nor set down aught in malice. Then you must speak of one that loved not wisely, but too well; of one not easily jealous, but being wrought, perplexed in the extreme; of one whose hand, like the base Indian, threw a pearl away—"

I stop. My throat aches.

Speak of me as I am.

Carlos never asked me for this, but Carlos never asked me for a lot of things.

I'm crying. I can feel the tears slide down my cheeks, marking me, making visible my grief.

I miss you. I miss you.

"Set you down this," I say, as Othello. "And say besides that in Aleppo once, where a malignant and a turbaned Turk beat a Venetian and traduced the state, I took by the throat the circumcised dog, and smote him, thus."

The rubber dagger hurts when it presses against my ribs, but I don't care. As I fall, all I can think is, *It's over, it's over, it's over.*

Backstage there is the hubbub of cast members milling around and tossing out congratulations, a hundred pats on the back, Max's high-five, Lacey's kiss on the cheek.

Then I turn and there's Prague, standing hunched over in a corner and looking awkward, hands tucked into the pockets of his baggy jeans. I walk over and Prague tilts his chin up in a gesture of greeting.

"Had a hole in your busy social calendar?" I ask with a crook of my eyebrow.

Prague shrugs. "Heard you were playing the lead or some shit. Figured I better check it out."

"Well, what's the verdict?" I ask.

"Othello is pretty badass," Prague says. "Fucked up, but badass."

Truer words have rarely been spoken. I give Prague a crooked smile. He's all right.

"I saw the photos you put up outside," Prague says. "They're for real, man. Carlos was legit."

I don't want you to be alone with that, Prague had said.

I wasn't ready to listen then, but I'm listening now.

"Yeah," I say. "He was."

I slap Prague on the shoulder, and to my surprise, Prague pulls me into a tight hug.

I see Tristan standing in a corner, alone. Did his parents

not even come? That's cold. I look up, and Tristan's eyes catch mine. His face brightens, and he bounds over to me.

"Amazing," Tristan tells me. "You were amazing."

"You were too," I say.

"Dude, of course I was!" Tristan says. "Did you expect anything less?"

Melanie wraps her arms around Tristan from behind and squeezes him until he squeaks. "My favorite whore-loving douchebag," she says.

"Now, that is not something you hear every day," Tristan says, and they embrace tightly.

When Melanie unwinds herself from Tristan's embrace, she wraps her arms around me and says, "You did it."

She means the play, but she also means something else.

We stand there in the middle of the chaos, holding each other close. I can feel her hand on the back of my neck, her hair tickling my cheek. She breathes, and I breathe, and we breathe together.

I did it.

I feel you, man, I feel you, I do.

AUTHOR'S NOTE

Three weeks before I began my creative writing master's program at California College of the Arts, my ex-boyfriend killed himself. I was the last person he spoke to. Though we had been broken up for about a year, we had dated for five and a half years and known each other for ten, and my sense of loss was enormous. Big enough for me to write a book about it. Big enough to define the next steps I took in my career. Big enough for it to still be hard to talk about, even now, years later.

Grief is complicated, and losing someone to suicide has got to be one of the most complicated forms of grief there is. It is a kind of loss that is overlaid with shame and guilt, and a kind of loss many choose to keep secret. The problem with secrets is that they're lonely. The more that people feel they can't talk about what or whom they've lost, the more alone they feel. It is always hard to grieve, but there is a reason we organize community rituals like funerals around death. It is hardest to grieve alone.

Grief is also complicated when you lose someone to an illness like cancer. It is no easier to feel someone slowly slip away than it is to lose them suddenly and seemingly without warning. *Grief will have its way with you,* a therapist told me once, and it is so true. We can't control the way we feel when we lose those close to us, or when we feel grief or how it manifests in our lives. We can't steer the roller coaster—we can only try to hold on.

But grief has things to teach you, too. My grief taught me a great many things, one of the most important being how essential it can be to reach out for help, even when it's hard. I hoped in writing this book that I might help people—including you, reading this now—to know that you are not alone. That your pain is valid and real and that there is a way through it. That it is okay to reach out, because when you do, you will find many people who are struggling or have struggled in the way you are.

Here are a few resources to help you with reaching out.

- **American Association of Suicidology: Suicide Loss Survivors: Books & Resources for Survivors**

    www.suicidology.org/suicide-survivors/
    suicide-loss-survivors

- **Alliance of Hope**

    www.allianceofhope.org

- **Suicide Prevention Resource Center: A Handbook for Survivors of Suicide**

    www.sprc.org/sites/sprc.org/files/library/SOS_
    handbook.pdf

- **The Trevor Project**

    www.thetrevorproject.org

- **ReachOut.com**

    us.reachout.com

- **SAVE—Suicide Awareness Voices of Education**

    www.save.org

- **American Foundation for Suicide Prevention: International Survivors of Suicide Loss Day**

    afsp.org/find-support/ive-lost-someone/survivor-day/

- **American Cancer Society: Coping with the Loss of a Loved One**

    www.cancer.org/acs/groups/cid/documents/webcontent/002826-pdf.pdf

- **Lifehacker: The Things Nobody Tells You About Grief**

    lifehacker.com/the-things-about-grief-nobody-tells-you-1383119181

- **It Gets Better Project**

    www.itgetsbetter.org

- **Susan G. Komen Foundation: Sources of Support for Family and Loved Ones**

    ww5.komen.org/BreastCancer/SourcesofSupportforFamilyandLovedOnes.html

- **Memorial Sloan Kettering Cancer Center: Caregiver Support**

    www.mskcc.org/experience/caregivers-support

- **Dana-Farber Cancer Institute: Family Connections**
  www.dana-farber.org/Adult-Care/Treatment-and-Support/Patient-and-Family-Support/Family-Connections.aspx

ACKNOWLEDGMENTS

This book was touched by many hands during its journey into existence, and I am endlessly grateful for all those people who helped me make it a reality. An enormous thank-you:

To all the young people I've worked with over the years who have inspired me and taught me so much about what it means to be resilient in the face of trauma, to survive and thrive in spite of loss. You and your stories are valuable and beautiful and amazing.

To my mentors and professors who helped coax this book out of me: Donna de la Perriere, Holly Payne, John Laskey, Aimee Phan, Rebekah Bloyd.

To my steadfast friends and supporters, members of Book Club both nearby and long distance, who put up with so much talk about this book and read drafts and believed in its potential even when I was ready to throw in the towel: Emily Rosendahl, Katherine Wooten, Anna Alves, Sarah Carter, Shana Naomi Krochmal, Jessica Maxwell, Erica Dessenberger, Siobhan McKiernan, Laurence Zavriew, Ash Rocketship.

To my fellow writers at California College of the Arts for their feedback and inspiration, with a special shout-out to Matthew Jent and Beth Mattson.

To my wonderful agent, Erica Rand Silverman, for sticking with this book through many ups and downs and ins and outs, and to George Nicholson for seeing potential in me from the beginning.

To my fabulous editor, Talia Benamy, as well as Jill Santopolo and everyone at Philomel Books for supporting and shaping this book.

To the Circle of Ancients, my grandparents: Big Mum and Just Ed and Grandma Shirley, for believing in my impractical passions, always.

To my parents, Amy and Warren Belasco, for their support and patience and love, and to my brother, Nate Belasco, for never letting me take myself too seriously just because I was writing a very serious book.

To Shannon Brown, my hetero-lifemate and my person, expert editor and reader and cheerleader. This book would not have happened without you.